The Secrets Beneath

Books for Adults by Kathleen Fuller:

A Man of His Word

An Honest Love

A Hand to Hold

Books for Young Readers by Kathleen Fuller:

A Summer Secret

The Secrets Beneath

Book Two: The Mysteries of Middlefield Series

by Kathleen Fuller

A Division of Thomas Nelson Publishers

NASHVILLE DALLAS MEXICO CITY RIO DE JANEIRO

Published in Nashville, Tennessee, by Tommy Nelson®. Tommy Nelson is a registered trademark of Thomas Nelson, Inc.

Published in association with Tamela Hancock Murray of Hartline Literary Agency, Pittsburgh, PA.

Cover design by Koechel Peterson.

Thomas Nelson, Inc., titles may be purchased in bulk for educational, business, fund-raising, or sales promotional use. For information, please e-mail SpecialMarkets@ThomasNelson.com.

Library of Congress Cataloging-in-Publication Data

Fuller, Kathleen.

The secrets beneath / by Kathleen Fuller.

p. cm. — (The mysteries of Middlefield series ; bk. 2)

Summary: Curious thirteen-year-old Bekah Yoder wonders about the strange behavior of the man who moves into the house next door, but even she does not suspect the danger that he brings to their neighborhood.

ISBN 978-1-4003-1620-5 (softcover)

[1. Family life—Ohio—Fiction. 2. Amish—Fiction. 3. Neighbors—Fiction. 4. Cousins—Fiction. 5. Middlefield (Ohio)—Fiction. 6. Mystery and detective stories.] I. Title.

PZ7.F955453Se 2010

[Fic]—dc22 2010026171

Printed in the United States of America

10 11 12 13 14 RRD 6 5 4

Mfr: RR Donnelley/Crawfordsville, IN/December 2010/PPO# 115820

To tweens and teens everywhere

Acknowledgments

I'D LIKE to give a big thank-you to my editors, MacKenzie Howard and Jamie Chavez. Thank you for your encouragement and expertise in helping me write this novel. I couldn't have done it without you! A special thank-you to my husband, James, for always being so supportive. Your patience and love overwhelm me.

A Note from the Author

The Secrets Beneath is set in the village of Middlefield, Ohio, in northeast Ohio near Cleveland. Established in 1885, Middlefield is the fourth largest Amish settlement in the world. Here Amish buggies share the gently sloping roads with "Yankee" cars and motorcycles.

Many of the Middlefield Amish, like the Lancaster County (Pennsylvania) Amish, are Old Order. While both the Middlefield and Lancaster settlements are divided into districts, each with its own *Ordnung*—an unwritten set of rules members abide by—there are noticeable differences in buggy style, dress, and cultural influence. In Middlefield, non-Amish are referred to as Yankees, while in Lancaster they are called *Englischers*. A Lancaster Amishman might drive a gray-colored buggy, while Middlefield buggies are always black. A Middlefield woman's prayer *kapp* at first glance might look the same as a Lancaster *kapp*, yet upon deeper inspection they are of differing design. There are also varying guidelines for the use of technology. While these superficial differences are evident among all Amish settlements, they do not detract from the main tenets of the Amish faith—a desire to grow closer to God, the importance of family and community, and living a plain and humble lifestyle.

With the help of some extremely generous Amish and Yankee friends, I have tried to portray the Amish in Middlefield as accurately and respectfully as possible. If there are any mistakes or misconceptions in my story, they are of my own making.

—Kathleen Fuller

Glossary of Amish Terms

ab im kopp: crazy
aenti: aunt
boppli: baby
bu: boy
buwe: boys
bruder: brother
daed: father, dad
danki: thank you
dochder: daughter
dumm: dumb
dummkopf: a dummy, or a jerk
Englisch: the non-Amish (Paradise group)
familye: family
fraa: woman
fraulein: an unmarried woman, Miss (when capitalized)
frau: wife, Mrs. (when capitalized)
geh: go

grossmami: grandmother
gut: good
guten morgen: good morning
guten nacht: good night
halt: stop
haus: house
hauss: houses
Herr: Mr.
kapp: prayer cap
kinn: child
kinner: children
lieb: an endearment: dear, sweetie
maed: girls
maedel: girl
mami: mom, mommy (Middlefield group)
mamm: mom (Paradise group)
mann: man
mei: my
mutter: mother
nee: no
nix: nothing
onkel: uncle
schul: school
schulhaus: schoolhouse
seltsam: weird
vatter: father
wunderbaar: wonderful
ya: yes or okay

One

"WHY DO ya always got your nose in a *dumm* old book for?"

Rebekah Yoder rolled her eyes at the sound of a boy's voice. Caleb Mullet—otherwise known as the biggest pain in Middlefield—stood over her. But she refused to look at him. Instead, she calmly turned the page. "Maybe if you read a book sometime you'd understand."

Caleb snatched the book from Bekah's hands. "Maybe I should read this one."

"Hey!" Bekah popped up from beneath her favorite tree in the backyard and rushed toward Caleb. She wished his family had never stayed for lunch after church. Then maybe she would have a moment's peace. "Give it back!"

He held it up over her head, flashing an annoying grin. Although they had both just turned thirteen, he was taller than she. He wasn't wearing his usual weather-beaten straw hat, and a hot late-August breeze lifted a large lock of his light brown hair. Chocolate colored eyes, filled with teasing glee, gazed back at her. "You'll have to catch me first!" He spun around and ran off toward the sparkling pond that edged her parents' property and also spanned to the Mullets'. She could see his house from here, and wished he would just go home—she wasn't in the mood for Caleb's annoying games. But she wanted her book back. She'd come to the part where Nancy Drew solves the mystery, and she couldn't wait to find out how it ended.

"Bekah!" Caleb had reached the pond and held her book over the edge. "Say good-bye to Nancy Drew!"

Fists clenched, Bekah ran to the pond. "Don't you dare, Caleb Mullet! That's a library book. If you ruin it, you're gonna pay for it!"

Caleb dangled the book above the water. Grinding her teeth, she picked up speed and hurtled herself toward him, ready to grab the book out of his hands. But just as she reached up he tossed the book over her head and onto the grassy bank behind her.

Bekah dug her bare feet into the grass but couldn't slow down. She slipped on the wet bank surrounding the pond and tumbled forward headfirst into the murky water. Stunned, she drew water up her nose. She broke through the surface, coughing and sputtering, touching her toes to the soft bottom of the pond. Her nose burned as she tried to steady herself. Then she heard Caleb's laughter. Wiping the water from her eyes, his guffaws battered her ears as he rolled on the grass, clutching his stomach.

"Woo hoo!" He gasped for breath. "That was the funniest

thing I ever saw! You went like this"—he jumped to his feet and imitated the way she'd tripped on the bank, windmilling his arms before pretending to tip into the pond—"and then you did this . . ." He cupped his hands around his mouth and let out a high-pitched shriek, which turned into a hiccup.

Soaked completely through, the ribbons of her *kapp* lying limply against her dress, Bekah wished she could yank Caleb into the pond and dunk him underwater. It would serve him right, especially if he got water up his nose like she just had. A fly flew around her head, but she didn't bother to wave it away. She glared at Caleb. "Shut. Up." When he kept laughing and hiccupping, she shouted, *"Shut up!"*

That seemed to get his attention. At least it quieted him for a moment. His lip lifted in a sneer. "What's your problem?"

"You're my problem!" She slammed her fist against the waist-deep water. Droplets splashed in her eyes. She wiped them away. "Look what you did to me."

He shook his head and hunkered down, his forearms resting casually over his knees, his face the picture of calm. "Don't blame me." He hiccupped. "You're the one who slipped."

"I wouldn't have slipped if you hadn't stolen my book."

"I didn't steal anything. It's lying over there on the grass. I just wanted to look at it for a minute." His lips curved into a mischievous grin.

"Oooh!" she exclaimed. He always had an answer for everything.

"What's going on here?"

Bekah shifted her gaze to the left to see her older sister Katherine and Caleb's older brother Johnny hurrying toward them. Caleb immediately leapt to his feet, casually shoving his hands in his pockets. He looked at the ground, kicking at a tuft of grass while whistling off-key.

Katherine put her hands on her slender hips, her red-gold eyebrows forming a V shape above her blue eyes. "Bekah, what are you doing in the pond?"

Bekah gritted her teeth. "I was bored, so I decided to jump in the pond and catch some fish with my bare hands." The sarcastic words were out of her mouth before she could stop them.

Katherine frowned, her left eyebrow lifting as it usually did when she was confused. "But, Bekah, why would you do something like that? There aren't any fish in the pond."

Bekah rolled her eyes and made her way out of the water. "I *know*." There hadn't been fish in the pond for years. Bekah felt a pang of guilt. Katherine wasn't exactly the sharpest person around, but she was one of the nicest. She didn't deserve sarcasm. *That* she should reserve for Caleb. She turned her gaze to him and glared.

"You had something to do with this, didn't you?" Johnny moved to stand in front of his brother. He was sixteen years old, the same age as Katherine. Unlike Caleb, he had his black, wide-brimmed hat on and still wore his black pants and white shirt from the church service earlier that morning, the sleeves rolled up above his elbows. His bluish-gray eyes narrowed. "What happened?"

Caleb glanced away from his brother's accusing gaze. "Uh, it was an accident."

Her dress dripping, Bekah shook her head, water droplets flying from her wet *kapp*. "*Nee*. It wasn't an accident. You did that on purpose because you wanted me to fall in."

"Did what?" Katherine went to stand next to Johnny. But she wasn't looking at Bekah or even Caleb. Her sister had been chasing after Johnny ever since Bekah could remember. Even with Bekah dripping wet and Caleb finally looking slightly guilty, she still had her attention on Johnny.

Johnny turned to Bekah. "I know you'll tell me the truth. What really happened?" He shot a skeptical glance at Caleb.

Bekah relayed what Caleb had done. "And when I went to get my book, I slipped and fell into the pond."

"See?" Caleb held out his hands. "I told you it was an accident. She admitted it herself."

"An accident you caused," Johnny said. "Tell her you're sorry."

Caleb shook his head, crossing his arms. "*Nee*. I don't have to apologize to her."

"You will apologize." Johnny moved closer to Caleb until he was almost in his face. "Now."

Caleb looked up at his brother, as if he wanted to challenge him. Then his shoulders slumped a little, and he stepped away. He looked at the ground and kicked at another clod of grass. "Sorry."

"I don't think she heard you."

"I'm sorry!" Caleb looked at his brother. "There, satisfied?"

Bekah didn't accept his poor excuse of an apology, but she kept quiet. It wouldn't matter what she said, Caleb would manage to defend himself. He always did. She watched as Johnny shoved Caleb toward the house, with Katherine close behind. She couldn't hear what he was saying, but from Caleb's grimace she could tell he was getting an earful. *Gut.*

Although the day was hot, she started to shiver a little bit. She looked down to see her dress clinging to her skin, water droplets dangling from the hem. She reached up and touched her *kapp*, which was soaking wet. Her mother would be mad when she found out about this. Bekah sighed. All she wanted to do was spend a peaceful Sunday afternoon reading her book. Leave it to Caleb Mullet to ruin it.

"Caleb likes you, you know."

Bekah gaped at Katherine as she sat on the edge of her bed later that evening. Just as she'd suspected, her mother hadn't been happy when she found out what happened at the pond. But at least she understood it was Caleb's fault. Katherine must be *ab im kopp* to think Caleb liked Bekah. "*Nee*, Katherine, he doesn't like me at all. Look what he did to me this afternoon." She ran a brush through her waist-length hair, which had finally finished drying. "And that's not the first time he's embarrassed me. Last year in school he stuck gum in my chair before I sat down. He's always yanking on my *kapp* strings. And right before summer break, he hit me in the head with a volleyball."

"I'm sure it was an accident," Katherine said.

"It wasn't, but he pretended it was, just like he did today. You haven't seen him play. He's very *gut*, and he knows exactly how to hit the ball and make it land where he wants it to."

"Usually when a *bu* treats you like that, it means he likes you." Katherine went to the mirror on Bekah's dresser and checked her *kapp*, adjusting one of the bobby pins holding it in place.

Bekah loved her sister, but she should have known not to expect her to make sense. "If Caleb likes me, he should be nice to me. You don't see *Daed* hitting *Mami* with a volleyball."

"Well, of course not, they're adults." Katherine giggled, and turned around. "*Buwe* are different. The weirder they act around you, the more they like you."

Shaking her head, Bekah said, "The last thing I want is Caleb Mullet liking me. And just because you've liked his *bruder* forever doesn't mean you know anything about *buwe*. If you did, maybe Johnny would start liking you." Bekah bit her bottom lip. That wasn't very nice. For the second time that day she wished she could take back her words. "I'm sorry."

Katherine joined Bekah on her bed. Fortunately she didn't look angry. "It's okay. I know Johnny doesn't pay attention to me. But that doesn't mean I'm giving up on him. He's the *bu* for me. I can wait until he realizes it too." She tilted her head and looked at Bekah. "If it makes you feel any better about Caleb, his *daed* was very upset with him."

"*Gut*. I hope he gets grounded. He deserves it."

"Don't be so hard on him, Bekah. *Buwe* are strange."

Bekah smirked. "So you're saying Johnny is strange?"

Katherine shook her head. A dreamy look appeared on her face and her pale cheeks flushed, making her freckles disappear. "Johnny is perfect."

Of course Katherine would think that. "Is he taking you to the singing tonight?"

The dreamy expression disappeared, and she looked away. "Um, *nee*. Not tonight."

As far as Bekah knew, Johnny had never taken her sister to a singing, although Katherine desperately wanted him to. She thought Katherine was wasting her time on Johnny. Sure, they had walked over to the pond together after Bekah had fallen in, but Bekah suspected her sister had followed him over there. There were plenty of other boys in their church district, and Bekah thought a couple of them might be interested in her sister. But Katherine only had eyes for Johnny. One thing was for sure, Bekah would never be that silly when it came to boys. "So who are you going to the singing with?"

"Mary Beth and some other friends." Katherine looked at the battery-operated clock on Bekah's nightstand. "Oh, I'm running late. See you later."

Bekah watched Katherine leave, wondering how her sister could be so excited about a *dumm* singing. She couldn't think of anything more boring than sitting around and practicing hymns all evening. But that was what young adults did, and a lot of them seemed to enjoy it. As for Bekah, she'd rather curl up with a good book instead.

She continued to brush her hair, picking up a lock and untangling a small knot out of the ends. She had the same blue eyes and fair skin as Katherine and their older sister, Leah, who had married and moved with her husband to Pierpont two years ago. The only difference was that Bekah's hair was closer to light brown than red. Still, all three of them looked similar. "Like triplets, but spaced out a few years," one of her aunts said. That same aunt also saw fit to give them labels: "Leah's the practical one, Katherine's the sweet one, and Bekah's the nosy one."

Bekah didn't know if she should be insulted by the description or not. She considered herself more curious than nosy. People who were nosy were usually gossipy, and she didn't want any part of that.

Bekah finished brushing her hair, then stood up and went to the window. She liked leaning against the sill of the open window, feeling the warm fresh air and contemplating the light blue *haus* next door. It had been abandoned for three years—after the Harpers, an older couple with grown children, moved to Florida—and its forlorn and faded black shutters seemed to proclaim its emptiness. She often imagined the type of family that would move in someday. Maybe they would have a daughter her age. But not a boy who was anything like Caleb, she hoped. That would be awful.

Bekah didn't know how long she stood there, her chin resting on her cupped hand, her imagination carrying her away. The sun had started to dip below the horizon, shining a hazy light on the side of the *haus*. Then she remembered her book. Nancy Drew had a mystery to solve. She grabbed it off her dresser and bounded into bed. It was so warm in her room she didn't bother with a blanket or sheet.

She had just opened the book when she heard the sound of a car engine outside. That was strange. They rarely had cars driving down their quiet country road. She set down the book and went back to the window. A maroon minivan pulled to a stop in the driveway next door. A few seconds later an old man stepped out of the vehicle. His bald head shone in the fading sunlight, a few inches of white hair rimming the back of his head. He wore a short-sleeved red-and-white shirt tucked into his pants, which were belted tight and high around his thin waist.

Bekah leaned forward to get a better view. This was the first time she'd seen someone at the Harpers' place. The man put his hands on his hips and rubbed his chin as he surveyed the front of the house. After a while, he disappeared around the back. She expected him to quickly reappear, but he didn't. Finally she saw him walking through the high grass in the backyard, the part she could see from her window. Usually her father kept the grass mowed or else it would get out of control, but he hadn't had a chance to do that lately. The old man didn't seem to mind the length of the grass, though. He just paced around the yard, staring at the ground. Then he walked back around front, got in his minivan, and left.

How strange. Why was he so interested in the Harpers' house? Maybe he wanted to buy it. If so, why didn't he go inside? If Bekah were buying a house, she'd at least want to see how the inside looked. But he only seemed concerned with the outside.

Maybe he wasn't buying the house at all. Maybe he was checking to see if anyone lived there. Her mouth dropped open. Maybe he was thinking about *robbing* it.

She shook her head. That couldn't be the reason. He looked too old to be a thief. Still, she should probably go downstairs to the living room and tell her parents that someone had been snooping around the house. But her father was probably asleep on the couch by now; he usually took an early evening nap on Sundays, waking up later on to take care of the animals. Bekah didn't want to disturb him.

Besides, what if the man returned? She didn't want to miss him if he did.

She waited for almost half an hour and then gave up. If he were coming back it wouldn't be soon, and her legs ached from standing up so long. She thought again about telling her parents, but decided not to. There was nothing they could do about it now. She'd tell them in the morning.

Bekah picked up her book and lay down on her bed. She opened the cover and started to read. Nancy had solved the mystery, but Bekah wasn't all that interested anymore. Her thoughts were filled with the mysterious man next door.

Two

For the next two weeks Bekah kept a close watch for anything suspicious next door, but the man didn't show up again. When she'd mentioned his visit to her mother, *Mami* just shrugged. "Maybe he changed his mind. That *haus* has been vacant for a long time. Some days I wonder if it will ever sell."

On a Saturday morning after breakfast, Bekah went outside to weed the garden in the backyard. She saw her father walk out of the barn with the push mower. She waved to him as he headed toward her. Snapping a long, tender green bean off one of the plants, she handed it to him when he reached her. He broke it in half and ate one part. "*Danki*, Bekah."

She nodded and knelt back down to weed. Thirty minutes later she finished the chore, and her father had finished the yard. When she saw him heading for the Harpers' house, she had an idea.

"Wait, *Daed*." Bekah rushed over to him just as he stopped at the edge of their property.

Her father turned around, his fair complexion ruddy from the heat of the day. His yellow short-sleeved shirt was soaked with sweat. He tilted back his yellow straw hat and wiped his forehead with the back of his hand. "*Ya*?"

"Are you going to mow the Harpers' lawn?"

He glanced over his shoulder. "I think it needs it, don't you?"

"I can do it."

His head tilted to the side. "That grass is pretty high, Bekah. Won't be easy pushing this old thing through it." He touched the triangular handle of the reel lawn mower, which didn't use gas power. "I'll go ahead and take care of it."

Bekah put her hand on the mower. "I really don't mind."

"Hmm. You've never been this eager to mow the lawn before." Suspicion entered his hazel eyes. "'Fess up, Bekah. What's going on in that curious mind of yours?"

Her mouth formed an O shape. "*Nix*. I just wanted to help you, that's all." *And find out what that old man was so interested in the other day.*

"I appreciate that." He released the mower handle and smiled, then removed his hat. "I do have more work to do out in the barn." He ran his hands through his damp red hair. "If it's too hard or you get too hot, let me know. I'll take over."

Bekah grinned and stood behind the mower. She pushed it toward the front yard of the house, where the grass was a little shorter and there wasn't so much of it. The house itself was pretty small and not big enough for a large family. It was one story, with a black roof and two concrete steps that led to the white front door. There were two large windows on either side of the door. The concrete driveway was on the left side, while on the right side there was a row of waist-high, thick green shrubs that ran alongside the house straight to the back. They separated the Harpers' property from the small open field on the other side. Bekah set to work, studying the house and the yard as she shoved the mower through the grass.

Before long, sweat started to drip into her eyes. Her father had been right, this was hard work. By the time she was finished with the front yard, she was not only hot and thirsty, she hadn't seen anything unusual. But she had to admit, the yard did look good.

"Nice job." Her father approached her, a glass of cold water in his hand. "Thought you might need this."

Bekah grabbed the glass and drank, the cool water sliding down her throat. When she finished she felt much better. "*Danki.*" She handed the glass back to her father and grabbed the lawn mower handle again.

"I think you've done enough mowing for one day."

She looked at her *daed*. "I can do the back."

"You look hot. Your cheeks are red."

"So are yours." With their fair coloring, she and her sisters and father's faces always grew red when they were hot. "Honest, I can do the backyard. This is kind of fun."

"All right, if you want to keep working, *geh* ahead." With a nod, he walked away.

Bekah pushed the mower to the backyard. Right away

she saw the grass was thicker and higher than in the front, and there was much more of it. Still, she was determined to finish the job and investigate the premises. Throwing all her weight behind the mower, she pushed as hard as she could, breathing in the sweet smell of cut grass. It tickled her bare feet as she went back and forth over the lawn.

Unfortunately, the back of the house was as boring as the front. A concrete slab for a patio, a plain white door with a metal screen door over it, and overgrown flower beds that she wasn't about to tackle today, if ever. Halfway through the mowing she took a break and stood in the shade on the patio. The cool concrete felt good on her bare feet. She looked at the flower beds bordering the house. They were filled with dead leaves, old mulch, and decaying weeds. Nothing interesting at all.

By the time she finished Bekah was not only hot and sweaty and sunburned, she was exhausted and disappointed. Whatever had caught the old man's attention when he had been here, she couldn't see it. The lawn mower in tow, she trudged to the barn and put it away, then dragged herself into the house. After nearly falling asleep during dinner, she went straight to bed when the meal was over.

By Sunday evening Bekah had lost interest in the Harpers' house and the old man. She had more important things to think about, mainly preparing for school, which would start the next day. She liked school and looked forward to it. They would have a new teacher this year, Ruth Byler, whom Bekah knew from church. She would also get to see her friends every day, instead of just at church or whenever they could get together. The only downside was Caleb—she'd see him every day too. But she didn't want to think about that.

She had just put her supplies on her dresser when she heard a knock on her bedroom door. "Come in."

Her mother walked inside and looked at the school supplies. A small frown formed on her lips. She made her way to Bekah's bed and sat down, patting the empty space beside her. "Sit with me, Bekah. I need to talk to you about something."

Bekah frowned, a little anxious. Usually her mother wasn't so serious. She sat.

Her mother shook her head, the lines around her blue eyes disappearing. "Don't look so worried, Rebekah. I just need to talk to you about a couple of things."

Bekah's brows rose. "Have I done something wrong?"

Mami smiled and put her arm around Bekah, giving her a quick squeeze. "You haven't done anything wrong. At least not anything I know about." Her eyes twinkled.

Bekah relaxed. "What did you want to talk about?"

Her mother let go of Bekah, her smile dimming a bit. "Your father talked to Gabriel Miller this morning at church. He's on the school board. It seems someone drove a truck into the side of the school."

Bekah's mouth dropped open. "What? How did that happen?"

"*Herr* Miller didn't give any details, but he said it was an accident, and that the young *mann* responsible is taking care of the repairs. But school has to be postponed until he fixes the *schulhaus*."

Bekah looked down at her lap, frowning. "When will it be fixed?"

"He wasn't sure, but he said at least a week. Maybe two." She touched Bekah's chin, causing Bekah to look at her. "I know you're disappointed, but these things happen."

"You mean someone ran into the school before?" Her eyes widened.

"*Nee*." Her mother smiled. "Nothing like that. But life doesn't always go as we plan it. God sees to it that we have plenty of adventures along the way."

"I don't see how driving a truck into the *schulhaus* is an adventure. More like a huge mistake."

"True, it was a huge mistake. And I'm sure the young *mann* learned a great lesson from it."

Bekah sighed and looked at the school supplies on her dresser. She had looked forward to using her new colored pencils right away. She could probably use them here at home now, but it wasn't the same. Having brand-new supplies on the first day of school was a ritual.

Then she realized there was a bright side to school being delayed. She wouldn't have to see Caleb.

"There's that smile," her mother said. "I'm glad you're not too upset."

"*Nee*, I'm okay."

"*Gut*. Now there's one other thing I want to talk to you about." Her mother glanced down at her lap for a moment, then looked at Bekah again. "Do you remember your cousin Amanda?"

"The one who lives in Pennsylvania?"

"Right. She lives in Paradise."

"*Ya*, I remember."

"She's coming for a visit."

"Really?" Bekah grinned. She had met her cousin only a few times when her family went to visit her father's relatives in Paradise. Since they were only two years apart, they would play together, and every once in a while they would write each other letters. But her family hadn't visited Pennsylvania in a couple of years, and she hadn't heard from Amanda for almost that long. Still, it would be great to have her cousin here. Despite having two sisters, Bekah sometimes felt like she was an only child. Her oldest sister was gone, and Katherine rarely had time for her anymore. She was always busy with her job as a waitress at Mary Yoder's Amish Kitchen, or spending time with her friends. It would be nice to have someone to hang out with again. "When is she coming? How long is she going to stay?"

"She'll be here sometime tomorrow." Her mother looked away for a moment. "And she'll be staying with us for the school year."

That was unexpected. "Are *Onkel* Ezra and *Aenti* Caroline coming with her? Are they staying with us too?"

Her mother shook her head. "*Onkel* Ezra is bringing her,

but he can't stay long. He has to get back to Paradise and take care of his farm."

"What about *Aenti* Caroline?"

Her mother paused. "She's not coming."

Bekah rubbed the back of her left hand, her enthusiasm dampened a bit. This didn't make any sense. She could see her cousin coming for a visit, but to stay for months during the school year? And why would she want to be away from her parents that long? "I'm confused."

"I know it's unusual, Bekah. But I want you to do everything to make Amanda feel at home here. You *maed* have gotten along well in the past. I expect that to continue while she lives here."

Bekah looked at her mother. "Why wouldn't it?"

Her mother bit her bottom lip for a second. "I'm sure it will." She touched Bekah's arm. "Also, while she's here I want you to introduce her to your friends at school. You know she can be a little shy."

"All right." Bekah had to wonder if her friends would want to hang out with someone two years younger than they were. But it had never bothered Bekah; maybe it wouldn't bother them.

"I'm hoping she'll make her own friends too," her mother added, as if she could read Bekah's thoughts. "I have to admit I'm a bit glad school is delayed. I think your cousin could use the time to adjust to living here before starting at a new school. Now, Amanda will be sharing your room, and your bed, since there's nowhere else to put another one."

Bekah nodded. She didn't mind sharing. "Okay."

"Before you *geh* to bed tonight, please empty one of your dresser drawers so she has a place to store her things. And remember how hard this has to be on Amanda, leaving her home to come here."

"I will." But Bekah had to wonder—if coming here was so hard for her cousin, then why was she spending the school year with them?

Her mother rose from the bed. "*Danki*, Bekah, for being so agreeable."

Bekah nodded, but she didn't look at her mother. Instead she thought about the situation. Normally, a visit from her cousin wouldn't be that unusual. But she now had her doubts. "Why is Amanda staying the whole school year? And why isn't *Aenti* Caroline coming with her and *Onkel* Ezra?"

Her mother looked away for a moment. A frown tugged on her lips, but it disappeared when she glanced back at Bekah. "Because she couldn't. *Onkel* Ezra has to get back to Paradise as soon as possible. He can't be away from his farm for long, so he'll be leaving on Tuesday." She looked around Bekah's room, which was a little untidy, as usual. Bekah was never able to keep it as clean as her mother wanted her to. A couple of books lay open on the floor near her bed, and her shoes were in front of the closet instead of inside it. The dress she wore yesterday was crumpled on the wood floor in the corner of the room. "You need to clean up before they arrive," her mother said.

"*Ya, Mami*, I will."

"I appreciate that." She gave Bekah a quick hug and told her good night, then went downstairs.

Bekah stood in the middle of her bedroom, letting everything her mother had said sink in. She wished her *Aenti* Caroline was coming. She didn't know her *Onkel* Ezra very well, even though he was her father's younger brother. Whenever they had visited Paradise, he usually spent all his time outside working the farm or taking care of the animals. She knew her aunt much better. Amanda looked like her. They both had dark brown hair, small green eyes, and almost permanently red cheeks that resembled the color of apples.

Questions continued to turn over in her mind. What was her *aenti* doing while her *onkel* and Amanda were gone? Who would be taking care of the farm and animals? Wouldn't it have made more sense for her uncle to stay home and her aunt to come?

Still turning the questions over in her mind, Bekah picked up the paperback books on the floor and set them on the small end table near her bed, which was pushed up against the wall on one side. Once she'd straightened her room, she dressed for bed, then said her nightly prayers. Only when she climbed in did she realize her mother never told her why Amanda was coming.

"Don't worry, Amanda. Everything will be all right."

Amanda Yoder looked at her father, who was sitting next

to her in the back of the van carrying them from the bus station. They were the last passengers left, the driver having dropped everyone else off at different stops on the way to her cousin's. Her father might have meant to sound encouraging, but Amanda didn't believe him. From the sadness and worry in his eyes, she could see he didn't believe what he'd said either.

She turned and looked out the window at the unfamiliar landscape passing by. She had never been to Middlefield; her cousin's family had always visited Paradise instead. Any other time she wouldn't mind visiting her relatives. But not today, and not for a whole school year.

As in Paradise, there were plenty of Amish homes here. She recognized them by their white paint, their shutterless windows, and the front porches and side yards that held laundry fluttering in the breeze. But the number of *Englisch* houses was different. There seemed to be many more here than back home. Some were made with fancy brick, or painted colors other than white. Many had one or more cars in the driveway.

Amanda fisted her hands until she felt her nails dig into her palms. She didn't want to be here. She wanted to be back home with her mother. But she knew that was impossible.

"It will be *gut* to see your cousin Bekah again, *ya*?" Her father put his hand on her shoulder. "I remember you two used to get along well."

Amanda nodded, but didn't turn to her *daed*. She felt his hand slip away.

"Amanda, you need to accept this."

"I can't." She faced her father, her stomach churning, but she kept her voice low. "I want to *geh* home, *Daed*. I want to be with *Mamm*."

"We've talked about this before." Her father leaned closer. "You can't be with your *mutter* right now."

"Why not?"

"I've already explained it to you."

"But I don't understand."

Her father sighed, pressing his lips together. "I don't understand it either, Amanda. But things are the way they are, and you're better off here with your *Aenti* Margaret and *Onkel* Thomas for a while, until everything is sorted out. Now, here's their *haus*. See, on the right side."

The van slowed down, passed a small light blue house, and turned into a dirt drive. The house was larger than she had expected. A front porch extended the entire width of the house. Small red, white, and pink flowers bordered the edge of the yard. At the end of the driveway she could see a small portion of the backyard, and caught sight of the end of the clothesline. A light blue dress that looked to be her size hung from it.

Her father paid the driver, then nudged Amanda. "It's time."

Amanda picked up her suitcase and slid across the seat as her father opened the sliding door. Her stomach hurt. When her father got out of the van, she had to force herself to follow him. As soon as she got out of the vehicle, her father looked down at her.

"Remember, Amanda. Don't tell anyone about your *mutter*." He put his hands on her shoulders. "It's very important that you don't. It's like a secret, one just between you and me. Promise me you won't say anything."

"I promise."

"That's my girl." He released her shoulders, his mouth tilting in a half smile. "I know I can count on you."

Amanda took her father's words to heart. And as they made their way to the house, she vowed to keep their secret, no matter what.

Three

"REBEKAH, COME! Amanda is here!"

Bekah fastened the last bobby pin to her black *kapp* and checked it in the mirror. She had pulled her light brown hair back, parting it in the middle and putting it up in a bun before putting on the *kapp*. Normally on a Monday morning, she would have already been dressed and at school by now, but that all changed with the closing of the schoolhouse. Instead she had spent almost the entire morning helping her mother clean the house to get ready for Amanda and *Onkel* Ezra's arrival.

Bekah stepped away from the mirror, intending to go downstairs before her mother called her again. Yet she couldn't help but take one more glance out the window of her bedroom, even though she didn't expect to see anything. Looking out the window had become a habit. Of course nothing had changed at the Harpers'. The old man who had visited that day had probably changed his mind about the house. Shoving him out of her mind, she rushed downstairs and walked into the living room, ready to greet her cousin.

When she stopped, she opened her mouth to say hello, but the expression on both Amanda's and *Onkel* Ezra's faces made her clamp her lips shut. Never had she seen her *onkel* so sad, and Amanda, who was sitting on the couch near him, wouldn't even meet her gaze.

Bekah's father stood next to his brother. Her *daed* was three years older and at least that many inches taller, but otherwise they favored each other. *Daed* tugged on his reddish-colored beard, his hazel eyes solemn and nearly as sad as *Onkel* Ezra's. Another strange thing, as her father rarely seemed upset, and she had never seen him sad. Bekah wondered if he'd even noticed she had walked into the room.

Her mother went to Bekah and leaned close to her. "Remember what we talked about, *dochder*," she whispered. "Make sure you help Amanda."

Bekah nodded and approached Amanda. She was probably sad to be separated from her family. Bekah knew she would be if she had to leave her parents and sisters for a long time. The only person she wouldn't miss would be Caleb Mullet. Not for the first time, Bekah wondered why Amanda was here. From the way Amanda's mouth drooped, Bekah wondered if her cousin were thinking the same thing.

Not knowing what to say, Bekah just looked at Amanda. Like Bekah, she wore a black *kapp*, although it was heart-shaped in the back instead of rounded like the *kapps* girls and women in Middlefield wore. Bekah twisted one of the ribbons of her own *kapp*, suddenly feeling uneasy. Everyone seemed either upset or nervous. Her mother touched Bekah's shoulder before sitting down next to Amanda. *Mami* looked at Bekah expectantly.

"Hello, Amanda," Bekah said, grateful when her mother's intense expression relaxed. "I'm glad you're here to visit."

But Amanda didn't look up or return her greeting. She kept her gaze focused on her lap, her hands resting on the white apron that covered her light purple dress. Bekah frowned. She remembered her cousin was shy, but not this shy.

"Amanda," her father said, his tone grave. "Answer your cousin. And look at her when you speak."

Amanda slowly lifted her head. "Hi," she whispered, then glanced down again.

Now Bekah knew something was very wrong. A weird feeling came over her.

"I better get going," *Onkel* Ezra said. He pushed his yellow straw hat lower on his head. He had the same red-colored hair as Bekah's father, but it was a shade darker, and his beard only reached a couple of inches beyond his chin, instead of resting against his chest like her father's did.

"You're not staying?" Her father looked at her uncle, then moved to stand in front of him, partially blocking him from Bekah's view. "You've just had a long bus trip here," he said in a low tone. "You know you can stay as long as you like."

Onkel Ezra shook his head, rocking back and forth on his heels. "I need to be getting back home. There's a bus leaving this afternoon. I don't want to be far from the farm for very long." He stepped to the side and turned and looked down at Amanda. He put a thick hand on her shoulder, and she stood up. When she did, he crouched in front of her so they were eye to eye.

"Now, you do what your *Onkel* Thomas and *Aenti* Margaret tell you to, all right?"

Amanda's green eyes turned glassy. "*Ya, Daed*," she said in a tiny voice.

"I want you to be *gut*."

"I will."

"And do your fair share with the chores. Don't expect them to wait on you hand and foot."

Amanda nodded, but didn't say anything this time.

He leaned forward and touched her face. "I promise," he said, his voice low and barely audible, "I'll be back to get you as soon as I can."

Bekah strained to hear what he said, but she caught most of his words. What did he mean, he was coming back as soon as he could? Wasn't Amanda supposed to stay here for the school year?

Onkel Ezra put his arms around Amanda, nearly swallowing her with his hug. She hugged him back equally as hard. When he tried to stand up, she wouldn't let him go.

"Amanda, I have to *geh*." Her uncle took Amanda's arms from around his neck.

"Please, *Daed*." Her voice sounded thick, as if she'd swallowed a spoonful of peanut butter whole. "Don't leave me here."

He touched her cheek, brushing his finger over it as if wiping away a tear. "It's better that you're here, Amanda. You know that. Don't worry, your *aenti* and *onkel* will take *gut* care of you. And you have your cousin Rebekah to play with."

Amanda looked at Bekah, but her expression didn't change. She faced her *daed* again and started to cry. "Please, *Daed*. I promise I'll be *gut* and help you at home. And you won't have to remind me to do my homework. I can make you supper and wash the clothes and clean the *haus* and take care of everything—"

"Hush, now." *Onkel* Ezra shook his head. "That's enough." He stood up, wiping his eyes with the back of his hand. He turned to Bekah's father. "I'd like to call for a taxi, if you don't mind."

Bekah's father looked at Amanda as if he expected her to protest again. But Amanda sat back down on the couch, staring at her lap. Her *daed* nodded at her *onkel*. "I've got a cell phone out in the barn. I'll *geh* with you. I have the numbers of a few Yankees who run their own taxi services around here."

"I appreciate it." He looked at Bekah's mother and nodded. "*Danki*, Margaret."

"No thanks necessary, Ezra. That's what *familye* is for."

Bekah couldn't shake the feeling that something else was going on here, something she didn't understand and that no one was going to explain to her. She chewed on her bottom lip. She didn't like feeling left out. But now wasn't the time for her to ask a bunch of questions, not when everyone was clearly upset. She watched her father and uncle leave, then turned her gaze to Amanda.

Her cousin's bottom lip trembled, but she had stopped crying. Bekah felt sorry for her. Her mother must have felt it too, because she walked over to Amanda and put her arm around her shoulders. "Would you like some cookies and milk? I just made some fresh chocolate chip ones. Aren't those your favorite?"

Amanda shook her head, keeping her gaze down. "I'm not hungry."

"Well, then, maybe you'd like to go upstairs to Bekah's room? She can show you where you can put your things."

Amanda nodded slowly, then stood, but didn't reply.

Bekah gestured for Amanda to follow her upstairs, wondering what she should say to her cousin. She had planned for them to play outside for the rest of the afternoon, and maybe walk down the street so Bekah could show Amanda the Troyers' farm. They had a huge herd of dairy cattle that roamed the fenced-in pasture beside the road. Usually when Bekah went there to visit the cows, a few of them would come to the fence and lick her outstretched hand. But now Bekah didn't know what to do.

They walked into Bekah's bedroom, and Amanda put her small suitcase on the braided rug in the center of the room. Bright light streamed through the window, making it lighter here than it had been in the living room. Bekah could get a better look at her cousin, noticing Amanda had grown a few inches since she'd last seen her. Her black prayer *kapp* was attached to her dark brown hair with several bobby pins, and a few wisps had escaped, framing her face. Instead of a straight part down the middle of her hair, the part was crooked. That was odd, considering how easy it was to make a straight part. Bekah looked at her cousin's dress and noticed a tear in the sleeve. It was as if she didn't care about looking neat. Bekah's mother would have never let her walk out of the *haus* with a torn dress, much less go on a long trip. Why hadn't *Aenti* Caroline sewn her dress, or at the very least helped Amanda with her hair?

Amanda noticed Bekah staring and looked away.

Bekah's cheeks turned red, and she quickly walked over to the dresser on the other side of the room. "Here's where you can put your things." She opened up the top drawer and pointed inside. "There's room for socks, underwear, and anything else. There's also space in the closet to hang up your dresses."

"I only brought one."

"Oh." Bekah didn't have that many dresses herself, only three, but if she were packing for a whole school year, her mother would have made at least two new ones for her. Amanda couldn't wear the same dress all year long. "Maybe *Mami* could make you another dress." Bekah clamped her mouth shut, realizing her words might make Amanda think Bekah thought lowly of her. "I'm sorry. It's just that I didn't think you'd want to wear the same dress for the whole school year." At Amanda's frown, Bekah inwardly groaned. So much for trying to make Amanda feel better. "I mean—"

"It's all right." Amanda lifted her chin. "I won't be staying here that long anyway."

"You won't? But *Mami* said—"

"My *daed* will be back for me soon, and everything will be fine. You'll see."

"Okay." Bekah didn't understand what her cousin meant, but then again she hadn't understood much of anything since her mother had told her about Amanda's visit. Bekah tried to lighten the mood. "We'll be sharing this bed. Just to let you know, Katherine told me I snore, but I don't believe her." She chuckled, but Amanda's face remained grim. She stood there, her hands clasped together, but she didn't say a word.

Bekah shifted from one foot to the other, wishing she could disappear into the floorboards. "Okay, well, you can put your comb and brush and pins on top of the dresser. There's a place in the bathroom for your toothbrush. The bathroom is down the hallway. Just make a right out of my bedroom, and you're there."

"I didn't pack a toothbrush."

No toothbrush? Who traveled without a toothbrush? Bekah's curiosity took control of her mouth. "Amanda, why not?" she blurted. "And why did you only pack one dress? And why is your father bringing you here and not your mother? And why did *Mami* say you're staying for the school year, but you just said you're leaving soon? What's going on?"

Amanda stared, then burst into tears. She whirled around and ran out of the room, the sound of her bounding down the stairs echoing in Bekah's ears.

Oh no. When will I learn to keep my mouth shut? Bekah dashed after her, following the sound of her sobs into the kitchen. Amanda was pressed against Bekah's mother, her arms around her waist, soaking her dress with tears.

"Rebekah, what did you say to her?" Bekah's mother had her hands around Amanda's shoulders, a bewildered expression on her face.

Bekah held her hands out. "I just asked her why she didn't pack a toothbrush." She thought about not mentioning the other questions; from her mother's upset gaze, Bekah could tell that admitting that one question was enough to get her in trouble. But she didn't want to lie, not even by omission. "And, um, I might have asked her a few more things. Like why she's staying here—"

"It's okay, it's okay, *lieb*," her mother said to Amanda, leaning down in front of her. She looked up at Bekah. "You should *geh* to your room."

"I didn't mean to upset her, *Mami*—"

"Bekah, please." Her mother's voice was low, but stern. "*Geh* to your room."

Bekah turned around and left, feeling almost as upset as Amanda. Well, maybe not quite. But she was upset. It wasn't like she meant to make Amanda cry. Besides, it wasn't her fault. If someone would tell her what was going on, she wouldn't have to ask so many questions. As she left the kitchen she could hear her mother comforting Amanda.

"It's all right. Don't cry. Here, have some milk. A cookie too. You must be starving after that long bus ride."

Bekah scowled. She could use some milk and cookies. She'd only had a couple of pieces of toast at breakfast, since she wasn't that hungry at the time. But she was hungry now, and she couldn't go get something to eat because she was in trouble. Meanwhile Amanda acted like a baby, and she got cookies and milk.

Okay, that wasn't fair. Bekah didn't really think Amanda was acting like a baby. She was acting mysterious, though, as were Bekah's parents and *Onkel* Ezra. That frustrated her more than anything. It was as if all four of them knew this big secret, and they were leaving her out of it on purpose.

She ran upstairs and flopped on her bed, letting out a long sigh. Then she rolled over on her back and stared at the ceiling, trying to puzzle everything out. After a few moments she gave up. She didn't have enough information to even guess what was going on with her cousin. She got up from the bed and went to the window, resting her arms across the ledge and her chin on the back of her hands. She still didn't know what she did wrong, but she wouldn't argue with her mother. Instead she'd wait a little while and go back downstairs and apologize. An apology could go a long way to smoothing things over with her mother and cousin. Or maybe her mother would come in and apologize. Sometimes she did that when she and Bekah got into an argument. Often their discussions were easily resolved.

Yet she had a feeling that wouldn't be the case in this situation. She sighed again and continued to stare out the window. It was a cloudless sky with the sun shining bright and strong. A breeze picked up, the air gliding over her forearms, a bit of cool relief for the hot day. A couple of robins twittered in the tree nearby, and she watched as they flew out of the branches and swooped to the ground, pecking at some tiny bug or worm they'd found. Moments later they flew away.

She stared at the old Harper house next door, then stood up, bored. Obviously her mother wasn't coming, so she should go downstairs and try to talk to her. And Amanda. Bekah was just about to walk away from the window when she saw a vehicle pull into the driveway—the same maroon minivan that had been there two weeks ago. Her eyes widened, and she leaned forward, forgetting about her mother and cousin. The old man was back.

He got out of the van, wearing the same khaki pants pulled high above his waist. But instead of a red shirt he had on a blue short-sleeved shirt with a collar and white tennis shoes. He slammed the door and stared at the house, just like he did the last time he was there. But this time he dug into his pants pocket and pulled something out. He went to the door. Bekah saw something glinting in his hand. She realized it was a key. Soon the man was inside.

Guess he bought the house after all. She watched for a few moments, wondering what he was doing inside. The windows in the Harpers' house didn't have curtains, but she still couldn't see inside from her vantage point. Bekah leaned forward again, her head nearly poking out of the window. She felt a tiny pang of guilt. She shouldn't be spying like this, but she couldn't help it. Everything about the old man seemed so mysterious.

"Rebekah!" her mother called from downstairs.

"Just a minute!" She waited a moment to see if the man would come outside again. When he didn't, she started to move away from the window. Then she saw the shrubs that bordered the far side of the house begin to shake.

"Come down here now!"

"Okay!" Bekah squinted at the row of bushes. They remained still. Maybe she'd imagined she saw something there. It could have been the breeze, she guessed. But just as she relaxed her eyes, she saw Caleb Mullet's head poke out of one of the shrubs. She gasped. What was he doing there?

"Rebekah! Don't make me call you again."

Bekah tore herself away from the window, knowing if she kept her mother waiting any longer she would be in even bigger trouble than before. She raced down the stairs, still trying to figure out why Caleb was hiding in the Harpers' bushes.

Four

Bekah met her mother at the bottom of the steps, worried that she would be more irritated than before because she'd been kept waiting. But her mother didn't look angry. Relieved and a little out of breath, Bekah said, "I'm sorry. I should have come when you first called me."

"What kept you?"

Bekah bit her bottom lip. Should she tell her mother about the old man? About Caleb? She couldn't say too much about Caleb, since she didn't know why he was at the Harpers' in the first place. She'd find out why later. "I think someone bought the Harpers' house. That old man is back again, the one I told you about last week."

Her mother nodded. "I'm not surprised. Your father said he heard at work that someone was looking at the place." *Mami*'s eyebrows furrowed. "Please tell me you weren't spying on him."

Bekah glanced away. "Um, not spying, exactly. I was kind

of bored up there, so I looked out the window and saw him pull into the driveway. Then he went into the house."

Mami tapped her chin with her finger. "I don't know, Rebekah. That sounds a little like spying to me." Her mother bent over and looked in Bekah's eyes. "Don't be so nosy. If and when we have a new neighbor, it will be important to respect his privacy. No more peeking out the window at the Harpers' house. Understand?"

Bekah nodded. At least she wasn't sneaking around in the bushes like Caleb.

Mami straightened. "I got Amanda to eat something. She wouldn't tell me what got her so upset. So I'm asking you." She lowered her voice. "She told you she didn't pack a toothbrush?"

Bekah nodded. "*Ya*. And she only has the dress she's wearing. She didn't pack much of anything else." Then she whispered, "Her dress has a hole in the seam."

"I noticed." *Mami* touched her brow with the tip of her finger, something she did when she was worried. "Bekah, I'm sorry I got angry with you. I wish *Onkel* Ezra wouldn't have left so soon. It's hard enough on Amanda as it is. I want her to feel at home here. Then she was crying soon after you went upstairs . . . I took my frustration out on you."

"It's okay."

"*Nee*, it's not. But *danki* for understanding." She smiled. "Are you hungry? I was about to make us a late lunch."

Bekah was starving, but she couldn't eat just yet, not until she went outside to see if Caleb were still there. But how would she do that? Then an idea occurred to her. "Can we have tomato sandwiches?"

Her mother nodded. "I just picked a few this morning."

Bekah tried not to frown. Her excuse to go outside was gone.

"But we might need a couple more. I know how you love tomato sandwiches."

"I'll *geh* get them!" Bekah dashed by her mother and through the kitchen, pausing for a moment to wave at Amanda, then flew out the door. She ran to the garden and pretended to be checking the tomatoes. But she was really looking at the Harpers' house. Caleb wasn't anywhere in sight. Maybe he had gone back home where he belonged. Which was good; she didn't like him hanging around here. But she wished he'd stayed long enough to tell her why he was there in the first place. She couldn't stand not knowing why he was hiding in the bushes.

She couldn't spend too much time waiting for Caleb to appear, so she picked two of the plumpest tomatoes and went back in the house, glancing one more time over her shoulder. She walked into the kitchen, expecting to see Amanda still sitting at the table. When she wasn't, she looked at her mother, who was standing at the kitchen counter slicing a loaf of fresh baked bread. "Where's Amanda?" Bekah asked, handing her the tomatoes.

"She went to sit on the front porch for a little while."

"I can *geh* get her if you want."

Mami put her arm on Bekah's shoulder, stopping her.

"She said she wasn't hungry. We'll let her be for a little while. She has to get used to us and used to the idea of staying here. Once that happens, I think she'll be all right." Glancing up at her mother, Bekah hoped for the same thing.

That night Amanda lay in Bekah's bed, staring at the ceiling in the dark. She didn't know what time it was, but she knew it had to be late. Bekah lay next to her. Her cousin Katherine had been right: Bekah did snore. But the soft whistling coming from Bekah wasn't keeping Amanda awake. Everything else was.

Rolling on her left side, Amanda faced the wall, the cotton sheet pulled up to her chin. Things were so different here. The sheets didn't smell the same as the ones on her bed back home. The mattress seemed lumpier. Even the chirping crickets and the occasional lowing of cows coming through the screen over Bekah's window sounded strange. She would never get used to it here. Besides, she didn't want to.

She sat up and reached for the white afghan at the foot of the bed. It was too hot to cover up with it, but she laid it next to her and touched the fringe on the sides. She had a similar one she slept with at home; her mother had made it. She wished she'd thought to bring it. But when her father had told her to pack for their trip to Middlefield, she had taken as little as possible. She didn't want to get too comfortable here.

Running her fingers through the fringe, she closed her eyes and remembered what her mother had told her when she was a little girl. "You're never alone, Amanda," she would say, usually right before they said their evening prayers together. "Whenever you're mad or sad or even glad, you should pray. God likes hearing from us. And when we pray, God always makes us feel better." Biting her bottom lip, Amanda wondered if God would listen to her now.

God, I want to go home. I miss Mamm *and* Daed *so much. Why can't* Mamm *be the way she used to be*? Daed *says I can't come home until she is. I know you can do miracles, God. Can you make* Mamm *better? Please*?

Amanda opened her eyes. Nothing changed inside. She didn't feel better. She didn't feel anything.

Tuesday morning Bekah set about to do her chores. Normally she would be going to school today and introducing Amanda to her friends. But since school was still closed, her mother had pointed out that Bekah had plenty of time to get her work done. Part of that work was tidying up the living room.

As she picked up the newspaper her father had read last night, she thought about Amanda. Her cousin had cried herself to sleep, even though she had tried to hide it by muffling the sound with her pillow. Then this morning she hadn't said anything at the breakfast table and had picked at her scrambled eggs and sausage. Bekah had caught the worried look her parents exchanged right before her father left to head to work.

Bekah had tried to help by asking Amanda if she wanted

to go visit the Troyers' cows. But Amanda just shook her head. Now she was in the kitchen with Bekah's mother, helping making bread for the week. Bekah sighed. Would her cousin be like this for a long time? She hoped not.

Focusing her thoughts on the task at hand, Bekah dusted the oak wood coffee table and matching end tables, and fluffed the sage green pillows that matched the couch and recliner. She was in the middle of sweeping the wood floor when she heard a knock at the door.

Bekah leaned the broom against the wall and opened the door. *Caleb Mullet!* She frowned, her automatic reaction whenever Caleb was around. Then she remembered what had happened yesterday and stepped out on the front porch and shut the door behind her. "Mind telling me what you were doing sneaking around the Harpers' house?" she asked, keeping her voice low.

The day was going to be another hot one, and she was already starting to sweat from the sticky air. She didn't have her *kapp* on this morning; instead, she wore a thin, dark blue kerchief, which did little to keep her head cool. Caleb wasn't wearing his hat either, and she could see his hair was damp at the ends, along with his shirt.

"Me?" Caleb pointed to his chest. Today he had on a light blue, short-sleeved shirt. His forearms were tanned from spending so much time in the sun. "I wasn't sneaking around."

"Don't lie. I saw you hiding over there."

Caleb's cheeks turned red and he glanced away. "Then

you had to be doing some snooping yourself, because I was in deep cover in those bushes." He looked at her again, his usual smirk planted on his face. "At least I wasn't almost hanging out the window spying on the place."

"How would you know that?"

"Anyone with eyes could see you. You'd make a terrible spy."

"Spying on people is wrong," Bekah said, fighting the pang of guilt she felt because she'd been doing the exact same thing—at least according to her mother. She couldn't help but look over at the house. The minivan was gone. She didn't even know if the old man had spent the night there, as she had minded her mother's warning and resisted looking out the window. It hadn't been easy.

"I already told you, I wasn't spying," he said.

"Then what were you doing, exactly?" Bekah crossed her arms. She couldn't wait for the excuse he'd come up with.

He shrugged, shoving his hands in his pockets. "Didn't have nothin' else to do. Thought I'd see what was going on around here." Caleb glanced at the ground, then looked up, his expression filled with what she was sure had to be false innocence. "We don't have school this week, and my friends are busy."

Bekah wasn't fooled. Caleb had lots of friends, although she couldn't figure out why he was so popular. It wasn't possible that they were all busy two days in a row! And it wasn't as if he didn't have a younger brother to play with at home. Although . . . Micah was only four years old; she could understand why Caleb wouldn't be eager to play with him. It would be more like babysitting than anything else, and Bekah couldn't imagine Caleb being a responsible babysitter. No, Caleb had to have a reason to be here, and boredom wasn't it.

She dropped her arms and put her hands on her hips. "I don't believe you. People don't hide in bushes 'just because.'"

But Caleb ignored her. "Can you believe someone drove a truck through the school?" He leaned forward, grinning. "I wish I could have been there to see that. That must have been something else."

"I think it's terrible. I happen to like school."

"Well, I don't, so I'm glad for the extra vacation." As he talked, he moved, angling his body more toward the Harpers' house.

Bekah could tell she wasn't going to get anything out of him about the bushes. "So if you're not going to tell me why you were hiding yesterday, why are you here now?" Even though their properties backed up against each other, Caleb had never come over before, unless it was for church.

"Um . . ." His normally confident expression slipped. "I, uh . . ."

Then she caught him glancing at the Harpers'. It was a quick glance, and if she hadn't been paying attention, she would have missed it. "Aha. I knew it! You *were* spying." She smiled, satisfied she'd caught him off guard. That didn't happen very often. Actually, not at all.

"Look," he said, shoving his hands through his hair. "All I wanted to do was find out why that old guy wanted to know where the Harpers' place was. He stopped by our *haus* a couple of weeks ago and asked about it."

"So? A lot of people get lost around here and ask for directions."

"*Ya*, but he was acting kind of weird. Like he was nervous or mad or something. Then I was outside later in the day and I saw him wandering around the backyard. Looked like he was talking to himself."

Bekah realized Caleb was talking about the first time she'd seen the old man too. She hadn't been able to see him in the backyard from her window, but obviously Caleb could from his backyard. "What else was he doing?"

"*Nix*. Just walking around, pacing with his hands in his pockets, looking down at the ground while he walked. Then he left. I didn't think about him much after that." Caleb looked at the house again. "Then yesterday I was out on my scooter and I saw him turn down your street. That's when I followed him."

"And?"

"And what?"

"What did you find out?"

He scoffed. "Like I would tell you." Then he looked at her. "What do you know about him?"

"Like I'd tell you."

Caleb crossed his arms. "I don't think you know anything."

"And you don't know anything either." Why was she wasting time with him? "*Geh* home, Caleb. I've got chores to do." She turned around and started to open the door when he stopped her.

"Okay, you're right. I don't know anything. I waited in those bushes until my legs turned numb, and all I saw him do was *geh* inside the house. Nothing else. Then I heard Johnny hollering for me and I went home." He took a step back. "Now you tell me."

"Tell you what?"

"About the old man. Sharing information, that's how it works."

"How what works?"

His dark brows wrinkled. "I don't know. Whatever it is that we're doing." He waved her off. "Just tell me about the old man, Bekah, and I'll leave you alone."

That brought a grin to her face. "Promise?"

"Don't look so happy."

"Nothing would make me happier." She clasped her hands together. "I don't know much more than you do. He's gone to the house twice, and the last time he went inside. You saw him do that. Now will you leave already?"

"Do you think he's moved in?" Caleb asked, looking over there again.

"Who knows? It's not any of your business anyway. If he did move in, he would be our neighbor, not yours."

Caleb leaned forward. "Maybe he shouldn't move in. Maybe no one should."

"Now you're being ridiculous."

"*Nee*, I'm not." He lowered his voice. "I heard the *haus* was haunted."

Bekah rolled her eyes. "That's the silliest thing you've ever said. There's no such thing as a haunted *haus*. You know that, Caleb."

He shrugged. "I'm just telling you what I heard."

"Who told you that?"

He moved his head back and forth. "I refuse to reveal my sources."

"I'm sure you don't have any sources. You're making this up."

"*Nee*, I'm not. I promise."

She crossed her arms. "Well, you should know better than to repeat gossip, especially when you don't know what you're talking about."

"And how do you know?" Caleb quirked a brown brow.

"How do I know what?"

"That it's not haunted?" He smirked, crossing his arms over his chest in direct imitation of her stance. "Do you have proof?"

"There are no such things as ghosts. That's my proof." Not that she needed to prove anything to him. She wondered who put it in his mind that the house was haunted. Probably his friend Melvin, who was always telling stories, most of them far-fetched and untrue. "Besides, I thought you were leaving. You promised, remember?"

"I promised to leave you alone." He dropped his arms and scrambled down the porch steps. "But I'm not leaving until I get a *gut* look at that *haus*. I want to see for myself what that old *mann* was so interested in." He walked barefoot through the lush green grass in the neighbor's front yard.

Bekah stood on the porch and watched him, shifting her feet back and forth. He shouldn't be over there. Especially if the old man now owned the house. What if he drove up right now and caught Caleb? Not that she cared what happened to him. In fact, it would serve him right for not only being nosy, but also being *dumm* enough to trespass. If she had a lick of sense she would go inside, finish her chores, and leave Caleb to his own devices.

But then again, what if he did find something unusual? Or suspicious? She couldn't stand the thought of Caleb knowing something she didn't. If there were anything going on next door, she should be the one to discover it, not him. Besides, she'd never live it down if she didn't. He'd make sure of that. She scrambled down the porch steps and followed him. "That's private property, Caleb," she shouted. "You can't *geh* over there!"

"No one's here," he called out over his shoulder. "Who's gonna care if we look around a bit?" Caleb disappeared to the backyard.

She ran to catch up with him. He was standing at the back door and had already pulled open the screen. "Caleb!" she hissed. "You can't *geh* in there."

The screen door resting against him, Caleb reached out and touched the doorknob to the main door, giving it a twist. "Hey, look at this. It's unlocked." He flashed her a mischievous grin. "I'm going inside."

Five

"YOU BETTER not, or we'll both get into trouble." Bekah glared at him.

He looked at her, his expression mocking. "Are you chicken?"

He'd always been a troublemaker and bullheaded, but she'd never thought he would invade someone else's privacy like this. "I'm not chicken. I'm using my brain. You wouldn't want someone coming into your house when you weren't home, would you?"

"It's just for a minute." He turned the knob again. "Like I said, who's gonna know?"

"Did you forget what happened to your sister and brother a couple of years ago—how much trouble they got into because they were trespassing?"

"That's different. That was an old barn, and they were hiding Sawyer in it."

Bekah thought about the runaway Mary Beth and Johnny

had hid in an abandoned barn near their property, which had eventually burned down in an electrical storm. Fortunately, no one had been hurt in the fire, and Sawyer did end up being adopted by Luke and Anna Byler. Still, Bekah had heard from Katherine that Mary Beth and Johnny had gotten in huge trouble, not only for hiding Sawyer, but for lying and being disobedient.

"It might not be the same thing," she said, moving a little closer to him, "but it's still wrong. If your parents or mine find out . . ." Bekah didn't even want to think about that. She glanced over to her house, saying a quick prayer that her mother and Amanda stayed inside. Without thinking, she covered his hand with hers. Both of them were holding on to the doorknob now.

He glanced at her hand, then looked at her for a long moment. He had a weird look in his eyes, one she couldn't figure out. Her palm started to sweat, and she was starting to feel a little weird herself when he looked away and shrugged off her hand. "It's fine. No one's here, remember?" But he didn't open the door, at least not yet.

"You'll get caught."

"Awww, Bekah. I didn't know you cared."

She wasn't in the mood for his sarcasm. She stepped away. "I don't care. Fine, *geh* ahead and get into trouble if you want to. I'm staying out of it." She whirled around and started for home. She had better things to do than deal with Caleb Mullet.

He grabbed her arm. "Hey, Bekah. Wait."

Don't turn around. Don't turn around. Just pull away from him and go home.

"Bekah, c'mon."

She faced him. "What?"

"Okay, you're right, and I'm wrong."

Bekah blinked. Was Caleb actually admitting he wasn't perfect? "I might have to write down this moment for posterity."

"Ha ha. Very funny. Look, sometimes I let my, um, curiosity get the best of me."

She could understand that, having gotten in trouble for being a little too nosy herself. But she wasn't about to admit that to Caleb. Instead, she let him continue talking. For the first time, he was saying something interesting.

"But you can't tell me you haven't been wondering what's inside this house all this time," he continued. "I know you better than that."

She looked away, but not fast enough. She caught Caleb's grin out of the corner of her eye, and she realized she'd admitted the truth without saying a word. *Ugh.* He let go of her arm and moved away from the door, letting the screen door slam with a squeak behind him. Then he walked a few feet away to the flower bed up against the back of the house, squatted down by the weeds that had overtaken the bed, and started to scan the area. "Maybe we'll find something over here."

She thought about reminding him that he was still trespassing, but she didn't bother. At least he wasn't going inside the house.

"Bekah!" Caleb motioned for her, but didn't look up. His focus remained on the ground in front of him.

Bekah hesitated, but the excitement in his voice drew her to kneel beside him. Then she noticed what he was looking at. The grass and weeds in the bed had been flattened into the shape of the sole of a shoe.

"There's a footprint. And another." He looked up, his brown eyes wide and filled with excitement. "Someone's been here."

"We already know that, Caleb. The old *mann*, remember?" Even though they were in the shade of the eave of the house, she wiped the sweat off her forehead with the back of her hand.

"Yeah, but why would he stomp around in the flowerbeds?"

"Maybe he was trying to see what kind of flowers were planted here. Or what he'd have to do to fix the beds."

"But couldn't he do that from the edge? He wouldn't have to walk through the beds to figure that out."

This was going nowhere, and she was starting to get irritated with him. "Maybe he has his own way of gardening, Caleb. Look, I'm hot, and we're wasting time here. I'm going home." Then her gaze caught something near the footprints, close to the edge of the house. She frowned and looked at him. "That's weird."

"What?" A damp lock of his light brown hair flopped over his eyes. He shoved it off his forehead. He seemed to always be in need of a haircut. He crouched down beside her, and she wrinkled her nose. He also needed a bath. But then again she probably did too, since she was sweating as much as he was.

Trying to ignore how close he was to her, she said, "Look at the rest of the flower bed. It's all full of grass and weeds." She pointed at the small area of dirt beside the footprints that had pressed the weeds down. "But that part isn't."

"It's in the shade." Caleb stood up. "Maybe the weeds don't get enough sun to grow here."

"Weeds grow anywhere." Suddenly forgetting how irritated she was with him a few seconds ago, she reached out and touched the cool dirt. "I think someone's been digging here."

"Have you seen the old man digging?"

"*Nee*. Did you?"

Caleb shook his head. "I saw him walking around, but I never saw him digging. He didn't even have a shovel." He wiped his sweaty forehead with the back of his hand. "How many times has he been here?"

"Two that I know of."

"Then maybe he's been here more than that."

"Okay, but why would he be digging in the flower beds if he doesn't own the house?"

With a shrug Caleb said, "I have no idea."

Bekah scanned the flower bed again. There was only one small spot of bare dirt, big enough to plant a couple of plants, nothing more. She got up and looked at the other beds, kneeling down in front of the last one. Caleb followed her.

"No footprints," he said, moving beside her.

"It doesn't look like anyone dug here either." She frowned. Why did the old man dig in only one bed?

Then another idea entered her mind, making her shudder and tense her shoulders. What if it wasn't the old man after all? What if someone else had snuck back here and dug the hole? Before the old man showed up, she had never seen anyone next door, but that didn't mean people hadn't been coming around when she wasn't home or while she was inside. She didn't like that idea at all.

Then she came to her senses. If anyone had been sneaking around, or if her father had thought there might be any danger, he would have warned her and Katherine about it. Her shoulders relaxed.

"Maybe it's haunted after all," Caleb said. He let out a fake sinister laugh.

Bekah turned around and looked up at him, squinting against the sunlight shining behind him. "For the last time, Caleb. This *haus* isn't haunted." Then she caught the teasing glint in his eyes. He didn't believe the house was haunted. He probably never had; he just needed an excuse to snoop. She should have known.

"It's still strange though, the *haus* being abandoned for so many years, don't you think? I wonder why no one has wanted to move in before this." He shrugged, and before she could answer, he walked away and headed toward the back door again.

Afraid he would try to go inside, she jumped up and followed. "Don't you dare open that door, Caleb Mullet, or I promise I'll tell my mother on you, and she'll make sure your *mami* knows you tried to break into someone's house."

"It's not breaking in if the door's open."

Not this again. Caleb had to be the most stubborn boy she'd ever known. She grabbed his arm and yanked him away from the door. "I said *nee*!"

Then he burst out in laughter. "Gotcha." His cheeks, already rosy from the heat, turned even darker red as he continued to laugh.

"What?" A mix of confusion and anger ran through her. "This was all a joke?"

He nodded. "You really thought I was going to go inside the *haus*, didn't you? I'm not *ab im kopp*, Bekah. I'd be grounded for a year. Probably more than that." He laughed again. "But it would be worth it to see the smoke coming from your ears like it is now. I got you *gut*."

Bekah didn't find it the least bit funny. The emotions from the last couple of days swelled up inside her. Her cousin's arrival, the strange way Amanda and her parents were acting, the thought of strangers hanging around the Harper house when she didn't know it. And now Caleb Mullet was laughing at her, again. A mixture of frustration and anxiety filled her heart. She turned her back on him, wishing he would disappear.

Caleb stepped in front of her, the laughter gone from his eyes. "C'mon, Bekah, it was a joke."

She swallowed. "Your jokes are stupid, Caleb Mullet, and I'm sick of them." She headed toward her house, but before she could get very far he jumped into her path, blocking the way.

"Look, I'm sorry. I didn't mean to make you this mad."

"*Ya*, you did." She looked directly at him. She sidestepped him, only to have him block her again.

"I said I was sorry."

She sighed, her shoulders slumping. "Caleb, *geh* home. I have chores to do." *And I'm tired of dealing with you.* Her mother was probably done with the baking by now, and would have started on the laundry. She needed to be there to help her hang the clothes on the line.

"I can help you," he said.

"It's laundry."

"I don't care."

Bekah rolled her eyes. She didn't know any boys who wanted to do or help with the laundry, which was considered a woman's job. "I doubt that." She stomped past him.

Caleb fell in step next to her. "When you're done, you want to go fishing at the pond?"

Why wouldn't he leave her alone? "There's no fish in the pond. And even if there were, I wouldn't go fishing with you."

"Bekah, I don't get you. You were fine a few moments ago, and now you're meaner than a tangled up dog. I joke around with my friends all the time. They don't act like such a *boppli* about it."

When she reached her back porch, Bekah stopped and turned to him. He thought *she* was mean? He was the meanest person she knew, and that included their teacher last year, *Fraulein* Fisher, who had made the entire class stay in for recess for a week because one student didn't turn in his homework. Even she was nicer than Caleb! "Get it through your thick head, Caleb Mullet. We're not friends. I don't want to be friends with you. Not now, not ever. And don't talk to me about mean—I haven't forgotten how you made me fall into the pond."

A smile twitched on his lips. "You have to admit that was pretty funny."

Now she understood why he was here. He didn't want to check out the house or help her with her chores. What he really wanted to do was rile her up, which was his favorite activity. And since he couldn't pester her at school, he had to do it here. Of course he was successful. He always was. No matter how much she tried not to let him affect her, he always did. "*Geh* away, Caleb. Leave me alone."

Stubborn to the very end, Caleb opened his mouth to say something else when a small, dark-green car pulled into the driveway next door. They both stared as it came to a stop. A tall, burly man got out of the vehicle, which had a large rust spot on the driver's side door, near the rim above the wheel. His hair was cut so short he looked almost bald, and he wore a plain navy blue T-shirt. Even from several yards away, Bekah could see the black ink of tattoos covering his arms. She frowned. She'd never understood why people put something permanent on their skin. The Amish would never do that.

Caleb moved to stand beside her. "Who's that guy?" he whispered.

"I don't know. I've never seen him before."

The man suddenly looked over at them, as if he heard them talking. His thick brows knit together, his square jaw tightening. Although Bekah didn't know who he was, he scared her. She turned and ran to her back porch, hiding behind the house, knowing she was now out of his view. She crouched down and peeked around the side of the house. She could still see him. Caleb followed her, crouching close behind her.

"He looks mean," Caleb commented, his voice low in her ear.

"You sound scared." She was scared too, but she wasn't about to let Caleb know that. He'd never let her forget it.

"I didn't say I was scared. I said he looks mean."

Bekah glanced at him. He was lying; she could see the fear in his eyes. But she didn't say anything. They were safe here at her *haus*. The man wouldn't dare come over here, would he? If he did she would run inside and warn her mother.

The man turned away and went straight to the backyard, much like the old man had the first time he stopped by the Harpers' house. But unlike the old man, he wasn't there very long and came around front again. He went to the front door, which was locked. He yanked on the door a few times, then let it go. He ran his hand over the top of his head and turned around. Then he trudged to the back of the house again. This time he didn't come back around.

"I bet he went into the *haus*," Bekah said.

"*Ya.*" Caleb's voice sounded thin, and Bekah knew he was thinking the same thing she was. If they had gone inside, they would have been caught by that man. And from the looks of him, they weren't sure what he would have done to them.

"Bekah."

Bekah jumped at the sound of Amanda's small voice. She whirled around and bumped into Caleb, knocking him back a couple of steps. That's what he got for standing so close to her. She looked at her cousin, willing her heartbeat to slow down to normal, pressing her hand against her chest as if that would help. "Amanda! You scared me!"

"Sorry."

Bekah took a deep breath. "It's okay." She fought to remain calm. "I just wasn't expecting you."

"What are you doing?" Amanda looked at her, then at Caleb with a questioning glance.

Knowing Amanda would be seeing a lot of Caleb once school started, she introduced him to her. "This is Caleb Mullet, Amanda. Caleb, Amanda's my cousin. He stopped by to . . ." She couldn't very well admit what they had been up to. ". . . say hello."

Caleb nodded at Amanda, then turned his focus back to the Harpers' house.

Amanda looked at Caleb, then back at Bekah. Doubt entered her green eyes. "Are you two spying?"

Should Bekah admit the truth to Amanda, and risk her cousin telling her parents what she and Caleb had done? Or should she hide the truth? "Um . . ."

"We're looking at the house because it's haunted." Caleb glanced over his shoulder, his mouth forming a wide O shape. "Very haunted."

"Stop it, Caleb." Bekah could see Amanda's eyes widening, not with doubt, but with a little fear.

"It is?" She wrapped her arms over her thin chest. Bekah noticed for the first time she was wearing one of Katherine's old outgrown dresses. It hung on her slight body. Until that moment she hadn't noticed how thin Amanda was.

Bekah gave Caleb a hard look, then put her hand on Amanda's shoulder. "Don't worry, Amanda. It's not haunted. Caleb doesn't know what he's talking about. You don't have to listen to him anyway. He's *ab im kopp*."

"I'm not crazy." He glanced back at the house. Bekah nudged him in the side with her elbow. Hard. He winced. "Ouch, that hurt."

"*Gut*. Now tell Amanda the truth." She mustered her strongest glare, and for the first time, he looked contrite.

"Fine." He faced Amanda. "I was just having some fun about it being haunted. It's not. We're just waiting for that guy to come out of the *haus*, that's all."

Amanda's expression turned from fearful to curious. "What guy?"

"He owns that car over there," Bekah said, pointing to his vehicle.

"So there's an *Englisch mann* in the *haus*?"

"A Yankee," Caleb corrected. "We say Yankee around here. Where are you from?"

Amanda's cheeks suddenly pinked, and she glanced at the ground, running her big toe against the wooden planks of the small back deck, which was only raised a few inches off the ground. "Paradise, Pennsylvania."

He nodded, clearly unimpressed. He returned to his post and continued watching the house. They all three watched in silence for a moment, then Amanda spoke. "This is boring. Bekah, your *mamm* sent me to find you. She's ready for you to put the laundry out on the line."

"Tell her I'll be there in a minute."

"Okay. But she said she doesn't want to come after you."

"What's your cousin doing here?" Caleb asked after Amanda left. He didn't look at Bekah as he spoke, but maintained his vigil.

"She's visiting for the school year."

He didn't say anything, and she let it drop. They continued to watch the *haus* in silence for a few more minutes. Caleb stood up. "He's not coming out of there anytime soon."

Bekah rose and faced him. He was right—whoever the stranger was, they didn't have all day to wait on him to come out. "Like I've been saying for the past hour, you're free to leave." She had to get the laundry anyway. She turned and headed into the *haus*, not saying good-bye to Caleb. Which was rude, but the way he'd treated her today, he deserved it.

She went downstairs where her mother was putting another load of clothes into their wringer washer. It was much cooler in the basement, but since their washer wasn't powered by electricity or gas, it took a lot of work on her mother's part to make it run. Her mother's fair skin shone with perspiration. She wiped her face with the back of her arm. "Where have you been? I sent Amanda to get you awhile ago."

"I was playing outside." She didn't look at her mother while she picked up the basket of damp, clean clothes. Technically, she and Caleb weren't playing, but they had been outside. Fortunately her mother didn't ask for details. As Bekah headed upstairs she said, "I'll be back for the second load soon."

"Don't make me wait on you again, Rebekah. You can play later after the chores are done."

"*Ya, Mami.*"

When she came outside lugging the plastic basket full of clothes, she halted her steps. Caleb was still there, standing near the laundry line. Would he never leave? "I thought you went home."

He shrugged, leaning against the wooden pole that held up the clothesline. The other pole was a few yards away. Two lines were strung between the T-shaped poles. "I thought I'd wait a little while longer," he said, shoving his hands in his pockets. His wild hair stood up, as if he'd run his fingers through it while she was inside. "If he leaves, I'm going back over there. I think there's something suspicious going on."

Bekah set the basket on the ground. She thought the same thing, but if she said as much to Caleb, he would never leave her alone. Instead she kept quiet and picked up one of her *mami*'s dresses, shaking it out before pinning it to the clothesline. It had to be nearly noon by now, and while the hot temperature was good for drying clothes, it only made Bekah hot and thirsty. She looked at Caleb, who was still sneaking glances at the Harpers' house behind him. He was trying not to be obvious about it, but not doing a very good job.

She continued to ignore him, hoping he could tell she didn't care whether he was there or not. Just as she was about to hang the last item of clothing, he moved to stand next to her, grabbing the pants leg as if he were helping her hang it up.

"What are you doing?" She tried to yank the clothing free, but he held on to it tightly.

"He's leaving," he said in a loud whisper. "Finally."

Bekah didn't move as she watched the man slam the front door behind him so hard the sound echoed in her ears. He hurried down the two concrete steps that led off the small front porch and stalked to his car. Then he paused, looking directly at them.

"Quick," Bekah said, a frisson of fear going down her spine. She didn't like this man at all. "Hand me a clothespin."

Caleb grabbed one from the cloth bag hanging nearby on the line. "Can he see us?"

"Some of the clothes might be in the way, but I'm not sure. Pretend you're busy helping me hang this."

He handed her the pin, and at that moment a hot breeze kicked up, sending the clothes flying up like a flag waving on a flagpole. The man had a direct line of sight to them both, and he continued to stare at them. Bekah hastily fastened the trousers to the line and grabbed the basket. "We should *geh* inside before he comes up here."

"He wouldn't do that." Caleb didn't move. His chin was lifted, but Bekah could see he was as unnerved as she was.

"Then you can stay out here and find out. I'm going in."

But before she could leave, the man turned and got in his car. She didn't realize she had been holding her breath until he had sped down the road, the tires making a squealing sound as he left.

Her mother came outside and stood on the back porch. "What on earth was that?" She stared at the road, but the car had disappeared.

"Someone was visiting next door," Bekah said.

Her mother shielded her eyes from the sun as she looked at Bekah. "What do you mean, visiting?"

Bekah didn't want to lie to her mother, so she told her the whole story, except for the part about going next door and finding the footprints. She also left out Caleb pretending to break into the house. Although she wasn't completely sure he was only pretending. She suspected he would have gone in the house if she hadn't been there to stop him. "The *mann* just came out of the house and left."

Her mother frowned. "That's a surprise. I hadn't heard that the house had sold yet, just that there was someone interested in it." Then as if she had seen Caleb for the first time, she turned to him. "Hello, Caleb. What are you doing here?"

For the first time Bekah saw Caleb rendered speechless as guilt flashed across his face. "I, um, I just stopped by to see what Bekah was doing."

Her mother nodded, but her expression remained stern. "Would you like a glass of water before you *geh* home?"

Caleb shook his head, getting her hint. "*Nee*. I'll be on my way." He looked at Bekah one more time before he ran through her backyard, past the pond, and through the field to his house.

Finally. It had taken her mother to get him to go, but Bekah didn't care, just as long as he was gone. Yet she had to admit the morning had been anything but boring, partially thanks to him. And she was surprised to find out he was just as curious about what was going on next door as she was. She would have never suspected that.

Her mother motioned to her. Bekah walked up the steps to the back porch, the empty laundry basket perched on her hip.

"Bekah, how long has Caleb been here?"

"An hour or so, I think. Why?"

Lines formed on her mother's forehead. "Does he come over here often? I mean by himself, not with his family."

Bekah shook her head. "This was the first time."

"Did you invite him?"

"*Nee*! I would never invite him over here. I don't like him at all. He's mean, and annoying, and he won't leave me alone."

She had expected her mother to be relieved, but instead she looked more disturbed. "Bekah, listen very carefully.

Except for church, Caleb isn't allowed to come over here. You two are too old to be playing together."

"We were only talking, I promise."

"Nevertheless, I don't want him over here without either his parents or Mary Beth or Johnny. Have I made myself clear?"

Bekah didn't know why her mother was so irritated, but she nodded. "I understand." As she followed her mother inside, she thought she heard *Mami* mutter something about talking to Caleb's mother. Bekah didn't really care; she was just glad she didn't have to worry about Caleb bugging her anymore.

But as she took the empty laundry basket downstairs, she couldn't stop thinking about the mean-looking stranger. She shivered, remembering how he had glared at her and Caleb. He wasn't like the old man, who only made Bekah curious. The stranger really scared her, and she knew Caleb had been frightened too. Why was he there, anyway? Did he have something to do with the old man? She didn't think he did, and the more she thought about him, the more nervous she got. She didn't want to see that man ever again.

Six

LATER THAT afternoon, after the last load of laundry was dry, Bekah started to take it down from the line and fold it. At one time she had shared the job with Katherine, but now that her sister was working so many hours at Mary Yoder's, Bekah had taken on more responsibility and chores. Which she didn't mind doing, except that today she couldn't help but look over her shoulder at the Harpers' house, hoping the stranger wouldn't come back while she was out there alone. Her mother hadn't seemed concerned about him returning, but then again she hadn't seen him either. Bekah didn't want to whine to her mother, though; she was thirteen now, too old to let her runaway thoughts scare her.

She unfastened a pair of her father's dark blue pants from the line, then looked up at her bedroom window. It would be nice if Amanda could help her with the laundry. But with the exception of coming to get her, Amanda had spent the morning inside and then had gone upstairs to Bekah's room after lunch. For a little while Bekah thought maybe Amanda had come out of her shell. She had seemed curious about the Harpers' house. Her opinion changed when she saw the flat look in her cousin's eyes as she barely ate another one of *Mami*'s delicious meals, this time chicken salad, carrot sticks, and homemade brownies. Bekah sighed. *Mami* had told her to give Amanda time, and she would. Bekah prayed for a double dose of patience.

She finished folding the laundry and took the basket full of clothes inside. After dropping the basket off in her mother's room, she went to the basement and grabbed a jar of canned peaches off the shelf. Supper would be ready in a couple of hours, but her stomach was growling. The cool peaches would make a great snack on this hot day. She had started for the kitchen when she heard her mother call out her name from the living room. Bekah stopped inside. "*Ya*?"

Her mother was sitting on the couch, sewing the sleeve of a light blue dress. Bekah recognized it as one of Katherine's old dresses, one that didn't fit her anymore. She wondered if her mother were fixing the dress for Amanda to wear. As Bekah walked into the living room, her mother put the dress on her lap and looked up at her with an irritated gaze.

Bekah suddenly lost her appetite. Without being asked she walked over to the chair opposite the couch and sat down, clutching the jar of peaches.

"Bekah, while you were outside finishing up the laundry

I had a talk with Amanda. She told me some bothersome things. Why did you and Caleb tell her the Harpers' house was haunted?"

Bekah gripped the jar tighter. "I didn't tell her that. That was all Caleb's doing."

"Regardless, now she says she's afraid to stay here. She practically begged me to let her *geh* back home." She frowned at Bekah, her lips pressing together in a thin line. "It took awhile for me to convince her that everything was all right."

"*Mami*, I promise, I didn't tell her the house was haunted. I wouldn't lie like that. I made Caleb tell her the truth. So she knows the house isn't haunted. I don't know why she would tell you she thought it was. Besides, when she left me and Caleb, she was fine. Not upset at all."

Her mother looked at Bekah, her frown deepening. "That wasn't the case when she came inside."

Bekah didn't know what to say. She glanced down at her lap. Why would Amanda tattle like that? And pretend to be upset? Did she just want to get Bekah in trouble?

"Bekah," her mother said, looking at her. "I'm disappointed in you. I asked you to help me with Amanda. I told you how difficult it is for her to be here. Instead, you spend your time playing with Caleb Mullet, who shouldn't have been here in the first place."

"But, *Mami*, that wasn't my fault. I didn't ask him to come over." Bekah pressed her bare toes against the wood floor. "And I want to help Amanda, but she won't let me. She hardly even talks to me. She wants to stay all cooped up in the house."

"Then you should try a little harder."

Bekah bit the tip of her tongue before she said something that made her mother even more upset. None of this was fair. It wasn't her fault Caleb wouldn't stop bugging her or that Amanda practically ignored her. Yet who was the one getting in trouble? *Me, that's who.*

Her mother's tone softened. "I'll speak to *Frau* Mullet about Caleb coming over here. In the meantime, find something fun for you and Amanda to do. She's very homesick, which is natural. Maybe you could play a game outside or swing on the swing set. Amanda might like that."

Bekah thought they were both a little old to be playing on the swing set, but she nodded anyway.

"Now, tell me about this *mann* who showed up next door. Did you speak to him?"

"*Nee*. I didn't. I know I'm not supposed to speak to strangers." *Especially mean-looking ones.*

Her mother nodded. "I'm glad you remembered that rule. Did anything else happen that you need to tell me?"

"He went inside for a little while, then came back out."

"So he had a key?"

"Um, *nee*."

"So how did he get in the *haus*?"

Bekah licked her lips. If she told her mother that she knew the back door was open, then her mother would know Bekah had been over there, and she would be in trouble.

But lying to her mother would make everything worse. It seemed like no matter what she did, she ended up doing the wrong thing.

"*Aenti* Margaret?"

Bekah and her mother both looked up to see Amanda standing in the doorway of the living room. Bekah scowled.

"Amanda, come on in." *Mami* smiled and removed the dress from her lap and set it next to her on the couch.

Amanda shook her head. "Could I *geh* to the barn for a little while?"

Bekah thought that was a weird request. She didn't spend much time in the barn, although she sometimes helped her father clean it. When she was younger she liked to bring their horse, Sparky, pieces of apple and carrot and pet Sparky's soft nose. But now she didn't go to the barn unless it was necessary. She didn't care for the smell.

"Sure, Amanda. You may *geh* to the barn."

Her cousin disappeared, and Bekah heard the back door shut. She also heard her mother sigh. Then she looked at Bekah. "Where were we? Oh, that's right. The Harpers' *haus*." Her expression turned grave. "I want you and Amanda to stay away from there. I don't like what I'm hearing about strangers lurking around there. I'll have to tell your father when he gets home. Maybe someone is finally buying that *haus* after all this time, but I don't want to take any chances, not until we know." She picked up the dress again, lines deepening on her forehead. "I should have been paying attention to what's been going on over there in the first place. Sometimes I'm so involved with my chores here, I don't get outside as much as I'd like." She put her silver thimble back on her middle finger. "Why don't you *geh* to the barn and find Amanda? *Onkel* Ezra says she loves to spend time with animals. Maybe that will be what she needs to help her feel more at home here."

Bekah wrinkled her nose. She didn't want to hang out in the smelly barn. Besides, she was still upset with Amanda. The last thing she wanted to do right now was be around her. "But, *Mami*, I was just going to have a snack." She held up the jar of peaches.

"You can have that later, after we eat." *Mami* was focused on her sewing. "I'll call you inside in a little while to help me fix the food." Reluctantly, Bekah rose from the chair. Her gaze landed on the dress *Mami* was working on. "Why did Amanda bring only one dress?" The question was out of her mouth before she could stop it.

Her mother glanced up for a moment, then looked down again. But in that short span of time Bekah could see the sadness in her eyes. "I suppose she forgot to pack more," her mother replied.

"Wouldn't *Aenti* Caroline have helped her pack?"

"Maybe they both forgot." Her mother didn't look up from her sewing. "Now run along, Bekah. And remember—keep clear of next door." This time she did look up, her eyes slightly narrowed. "If you see anyone over there, you and Amanda come inside right away and let me know."

"*Ya, Mami.*" Bekah left the living room and went to the

kitchen. She realized her mother hadn't answered her question. This was the second time *Mami* had done this, and Bekah didn't know what to think. She set the jar of peaches on the counter near the sink, ignoring her growling stomach. She should have had double helpings of *Mami*'s chicken salad at lunch.

She walked out the back door of the kitchen and went straight to the barn, sneaking a glance at the Harpers' house. The driveway was empty, and so was the backyard. She had to admit she was kind of glad her mother warned her to stay away from the house. She didn't want to risk running into that stranger again.

When Bekah entered the barn, she saw Amanda standing on her tiptoes in front of Sparky's stall, reaching up and touching the horse's nose with her fingertip. Bekah breathed in the stinky smell of hay and horse. She thought her cousin had heard her walk in, and waited for her to turn around. When she didn't, she called out her name. "Amanda."

Her cousin jumped, much like Bekah had done when Amanda had startled her earlier. *Serves her right*. Bekah tried to get rid of the mean thought, but it wouldn't go away. Amanda hadn't lived with them for very long, but she was already starting to get on Bekah's nerves.

"I don't appreciate you tattling on me."

Amanda turned around and faced her. "I didn't tattle. You both said the house was haunted. I don't want to live next to a haunted *haus*. So I told your *mamm* about it."

"And thanks to you, I got in trouble."

"That's not my fault."

"*Ya*, it is." Bekah walked up to her. "I don't know what your problem is, but you had to know that would get me in trouble. You also knew that Caleb admitted it wasn't haunted. So you not only got me in trouble, you told a lie."

Amanda's lower lip quivered, and she looked at Sparky again. She tugged on one of the black strings of her *kapp*. "I wasn't sure if I could believe him or not."

Bekah sighed. She could sympathize with her cousin's confusion over Caleb. Bekah had spent the past couple of years being confused herself. "Look, it doesn't matter anymore. I just don't want you to believe that the *haus* is haunted. Because it isn't."

"Caleb said it was."

"Don't listen to Caleb. I don't. He was being *dumm*; he's always like that."

"But why would he say it was haunted if it wasn't?"

"Because he's Caleb, and he lives to rile people up, especially me. I think he just said that to see what your reaction would be." It dawned on Bekah that this was the longest conversation they'd had since Amanda had arrived. Maybe they were making progress after all. "There's nothing wrong with that house next door." *At least not until today*. But she didn't want to mention anything about the stranger, not when Amanda was already spooked about what Caleb had said.

"If there's nothing wrong with the *haus*, then why were you and Caleb spying on it?"

"We were messing around." Bekah kept the details to herself. "It doesn't matter anyway. Caleb won't be coming around here anymore, and I'm not paying any more attention to what goes on next door. Besides, *Mami* said we need to stay away from there."

Amanda looked at her, her brows lifting. "Because I told her I thought it was haunted?"

"*Nee*, because someone might have bought the *haus*, and we don't have any business being over there."

"Oh." Amanda turned around and started petting Sparky's nose again.

Bekah went to stand next to her cousin. "She likes that. She hasn't been feeling well lately. *Daed* says she has a sore foot."

"That's too bad." After a pause, Amanda asked, "Does she like apples?"

"*Ya*. Carrots too. All horses like those things."

"Our horse likes hot dogs."

"Really?" Bekah had never heard of a horse eating hot dogs. She thought they only ate vegetables, fruit, and grain. "That's *seltsam*."

"But *Daed* said not to give them to him, because they'll mess up Abner's stomach. Our other horse, Black Beauty, doesn't like them. *Daed* said that's because he's normal and Abner's not." She glanced at Bekah. "But I love them both the same."

"Black Beauty—is that the same as the book?"

Amanda nodded. "*Daed* said I could name him. He looks

just like the horse in the story, solid black all over." Her face fell. "I miss him very much."

Bekah wasn't sure if Amanda was talking about her father or the horse, but she suspected both.

Amanda sighed. "I didn't mean to get you in trouble, Bekah. I'm sorry."

Amanda's apology sparked another pang of guilt. Every time Bekah started to get upset with Amanda, her cousin said something that made her feel guilty. "It's okay." Bekah patted Sparky on the nose. Remembering what her mother said about trying to get Amanda to do things, she asked, "Would you like to *geh* swing on the swing set?"

Amanda shook her head. She leaned her forearms on top of the stall door and stared at the horse.

"Okay, no swinging then. What about a game of Frisbee?"

"I'd just like to be alone, if that's okay."

Bekah frowned. Her mother wouldn't think that was okay, but what else could Bekah do? She couldn't force Amanda to play with her. She had to admit it hurt her feelings a little bit that her cousin didn't want to do anything with her. But she shrugged as if it didn't matter. "Suit yourself. I'm going inside." When Amanda didn't respond, Bekah hurried out the door, glad for the fresh air.

If she doesn't want to do anything with me, so be it. Although she'd told Amanda she was going inside, she couldn't. Her mother would ask her why she wasn't with Amanda, and Bekah didn't feel like explaining that her cousin had rejected her—again. Instead Bekah walked down to the

Troyers' property. When she reached the fence, three of the huge black-and-white cows sauntered over to her, sticking out their long, grayish tongues. She touched the top of one cow's damp nose, and the cow nudged against the fence, as if wanting more attention. *At least someone around here likes me.*

Amanda let out a deep breath. She suspected she'd hurt her cousin's feelings, but she couldn't help it. She didn't want to swing or play Frisbee or do anything fun. She also hadn't meant to get Bekah into trouble. Amanda knew the house wasn't haunted, but she thought if she told her aunt that she thought it was and that she was scared, they would take her back to Paradise. That plan hadn't worked out at all. She was still here, and now Bekah was irritated with her. Her cousin tried to hide it, but Amanda could tell.

But she couldn't worry about how Bekah felt. She had to figure out a way to get home. Standing in the barn made her homesickness worse, but it also comforted her. What were Abner and Black Beauty doing right now? They probably had their noses to the ground in *Daed*'s pasture, eating the tender grasses as their thick tails swished at the flies buzzing around them. She missed the horses so much. And her calico cat, Paw-Paw. *Daed* had told her Paw-Paw would be fine without her, but Amanda still worried. What if Paw-Paw was lonely too? Would *Daed* know to scratch behind Paw-Paw's ears three times each? Amanda shook her head.

She knew *Daed* was too busy with everything to think about Paw-Paw.

She felt something soft brush against her ankles. Surprised, she looked down to see a black-and-white dog sit down by her feet. He looked up and barked at her.

"Hello there." Amanda knelt down and rubbed the top of the dog's head. She didn't know Bekah had a dog. No one had mentioned him, and this was the first time Amanda had seen him. Maybe he was a stray—but he sure was a well-kept one. He was a cute dog, with thick, soft fur. She petted him for a while, and when she stopped, he licked her hand. That made her smile.

"You're a *gut bu*, aren't you? Let's *geh* see if we can find you something to eat." Maybe *Aenti* Margaret had some left-over meat or a piece of cheese she'd let Amanda give to the dog. He trotted beside her as they left the barn. But when she headed for the house, he set off toward the neighbors, the house Bekah and Caleb were watching earlier.

"Hey!" she called, going after him. "Come back!"

But the dog picked up speed until he was in the neighbor's backyard. He came to a stop in the middle, then turned around and sat on his haunches. His red tongue lolled out of the side of his mouth.

"Doggie?" Amanda halted her steps at the edge of the yard, remembering that she wasn't supposed to go over there. She called for the dog a couple more times. He sat and looked at her, then turned around and went in the opposite direction.

Amanda sighed. Everyone always went away. Her mother.

Her father. Now the dog. She was all alone, and she was tired of it. She stood there, trying to figure out what to do. She didn't want to be alone anymore. A few minutes later she realized she didn't have to be. Her decision made, she left the barn and went back in the house, hoping her aunt, uncle, and Bekah would someday forgive her for what she was about to do.

After Bekah grew tired of the Troyers' cows, she returned home. She checked the barn to see if Amanda was still there. When she found the barn empty, she left for the house. When she walked into the kitchen, she saw her mother standing at the counter. *Mami* pulled a large baking pan from the cupboard underneath the counter.

"Have you seen Amanda?" Bekah asked.

"She came in a little while ago and went upstairs." Her mother turned on the oven. "We'll call her down when it's time to eat."

"What's for supper?"

"Chicken and rice casserole."

Bekah made a face. She didn't like that casserole. Chicken and rice were okay separately, but her mother put them together and poured a can of cream of mushroom soup on top. Blech.

Her mother looked at her, sympathy in her eyes. "I know you don't care for it, but it's one of Amanda's favorites. You can eat a little bit for her sake. I thought if I made something she liked, she would eat a little bit more. I tried to get her to help me prepare supper, but she said she wanted to *geh* upstairs instead."

Guilt nudged Bekah again. She shook it off. If Amanda wanted to stay upstairs that was her business. Instead, Bekah focused on helping with supper. Then she found out that in addition to the dreaded chicken and rice, they were also having cooked cabbage, another dish she didn't like. "Will Katherine be home in time for supper?" she asked hopefully. Sometimes her sister brought home food from Mary Yoder's when she was finished from her shift. Bekah could eat that instead.

Her mother shook her head. "*Nee*. She's working until eight tonight."

Bekah tried to hide her disappointment. She knew she should be grateful for the food, not complaining about it. She sighed. "What can I help you with?"

Her mother smiled and put her arms around Bekah's shoulders. "*Danki*, Bekah, for understanding and going along with all of this. As hard as things are on Amanda, I know they're not easy for you. And I know chicken and rice isn't your favorite."

Her mother's understanding perked her up a bit. "That's okay, *Mami*. I'm sure Amanda will like the meal."

"I hope so." *Mami* gave Bekah another squeeze and walked over to the stove. "And just so you don't think I've forgotten about you, we're having your favorite vegetable—brown-sugar carrots. Plus, there'll be extra biscuits."

Bekah grinned, feeling much better now. The meal wouldn't be so bad after all. "I'll peel the carrots," she said.

Almost an hour later, supper was finished and her father had come home from his construction job. He walked into the kitchen and took off his yellow straw hat, breathing in deeply—chicken and rice was also one of his favorite meals. "Smells *gut*!" He walked over and touched his wife's shoulder, peering down at the pot of cooked carrots on the stove. "I'm starving."

Her mother chuckled and sent him away. "*Geh* wash up, we'll be serving the food soon."

"I have to check on Sparky first. I want to make sure her foot is healing." At *Mami*'s grimace, her father added, "It will only take me a minute."

When *Daed* left, her mother turned to Bekah. "Run upstairs and tell Amanda it's time to eat. Your father should be back by the time you both wash up."

Bekah nodded and went to her bedroom. But when she peered inside, she didn't see Amanda. She frowned and checked her parents' bedroom, then Katherine's. No Amanda. "Amanda?" When she didn't answer Bekah ran through the rooms downstairs.

"*Mami*, have you seen Amanda?" she asked, bursting into the kitchen.

Her mother's eyes grew wide. "*Nee*. I thought she was upstairs in your room."

"She's not. I checked every room upstairs. Down here too."

"What about the basement?"

She had forgotten about the basement. "I'll be right back."

But a few moments later, she returned. "*Mami*, Amanda's not in the *haus*."

Her mother picked up two potholders, then opened the oven door. "Then she must have gone back to the barn."

"Who's in the barn?" Bekah's father came inside the kitchen.

"Amanda. She asked to *geh* out there earlier." *Mami* pulled out the casserole dish and placed it on the counter. Swirls of steam rose from the creamy rice dish.

Daed frowned. "*Nee*, she's not. I was just out there and I didn't see her."

A thread of panic wound through Bekah. She looked at her mother and saw worry reflected in her face. Then Bekah realized what must have happened: Amanda had run away.

Seven

AMANDA WALKED down the road, not sure where she was going . . . but she didn't care. All she wanted to do was leave Middlefield. She couldn't stay here anymore. Her horses needed her. Paw-Paw needed her. And her father needed her most of all.

She thought about the twenty-dollar bill tucked in her knee sock. Her father had given her the money right before he left to go back to Paradise, telling her it was for an emergency. Well, this was an emergency. Somehow she had to find the bus station. She wished she'd paid more attention to the roads and directions on the way here. But she'd thought he would change his mind—she had never believed her father would truly leave her. But he did, and now she was stuck here. Alone.

Her eyes started to sting, and she rubbed at them with the back of her hand. She wouldn't cry. Her father had told her not to cry, that she had to be strong, and she had tried to be for weeks, ever since her mother had left her and her father in Paradise. But it was getting harder to ignore the pain in her heart. Her father had also told her to rely on the Lord whenever she felt lonely. But that didn't help either. She prayed every night, each time harder than the last, and the ache in her chest grew bigger and hurt a lot more. God didn't listen to her. He didn't care how she felt or what happened to her. If he did, he would have stopped her mother from leaving the family. They would all be together, the way they were supposed to be.

She made a right turn on a road called Bundysburg and continued to walk. She had changed into her old dress and left the one her *aenti* had let her wear hanging in the closet in Bekah's room. It wasn't that she didn't appreciate what her aunt and uncle had done for her. They were both very kind, and she didn't want to hurt their feelings. But she didn't belong here. She belonged back in Paradise with her father. He'd said he couldn't take care of her like she needed, not while *Mamm* was gone. But that wasn't true. They had done just fine on their own during the summer, just the two of them.

But maybe he didn't want her. Just like her mother hadn't wanted her.

She swallowed the lump that formed in her throat. As she walked, cars passed her by, none of them stopping. It was late afternoon, but the sun beat down on her head, the heat searing through her black prayer *kapp*. Sweat dripped down the side of her face, but she didn't bother to wipe it away. Her mouth was dry too. She hoped she had enough money to buy a bus ticket once she found the station, and a cold drink too. She continued to the end of the road, hearing more cars and seeing a few more buggies out. A white-and-black sign was situated a few feet before the red stop sign. It had the number 87 on it. She had no idea what that meant, but considering the amount of traffic passing by, she could see she was nearing a major road. That had to take her to the bus station.

She was just about to turn again when she heard someone call her name. "Amanda!"

She looked over her shoulder and saw Bekah's head poking out of a buggy. Her father was in the driver's seat, and she saw him tap on the back of the horse with his reins. Alarm spread through her. What could she do now? She couldn't outrun a horse. She thought about trying to anyway, but her indecision paralyzed her, making her stand in place. By that time the buggy had reached the corner, pulling up beside her.

"Where are you going?" Bekah looked both confused and upset at the same time. Her uncle just looked angry.

Amanda figured she had nothing to lose by telling the truth. "Home. I just want to go home."

"Then get in the buggy and we'll take you home."

She shook her head. "That's not my home. I want to go back to Paradise."

A car horn honked behind the buggy. Amanda looked at the car, seeing the driver's angry face through the windshield.

"How are you going to do that?" Bekah asked.

"I'll take the bus. I have some money, so I can get a ticket."

Her uncle leaned forward, peering over Bekah's shoulder. "You're going the wrong way to the bus station, Amanda. And you can't walk there; it's too far." His voice was gentle, as it usually was, but his look was stern. "We can't sit here all day, Amanda. Get in the buggy, right now. We'll talk about this when we get back to the *haus*."

Amanda hesitated for a moment, knowing the longer she waited, the more trouble she would be in. She didn't have a choice. She couldn't outrun a buggy, and the driver in the car behind her uncle's buggy honked his horn again. Reluctantly, she got in the buggy and sat by Bekah, who still looked bewildered.

Onkel Thomas turned right on the main road, slapping the reins against the horse's back flanks. Amanda remembered Bekah telling her Sparky had a sore foot. Now she felt bad for the horse, noticing how slowly she walked. Amanda looked straight ahead, her stomach bundled into a knot. She didn't want to look at her uncle's face, afraid of what she might see. If she had done something like this to her father, he would ground her for a month.

A few moments of silence passed. Finally, Bekah spoke. "Why did you run away, Amanda?" She sounded hurt.

"I wasn't running away. I was going back to where I belong." She looked outside the window of the buggy at the wide-open fields, white Amish houses, and the cars and buggies traveling down the road as Sparky made her way back to Amanda's aunt and uncle's house. It hurt to swallow. She was trapped here, and there was nothing she could do about it.

She turned away from Bekah and her father, keeping her mouth shut. Nobody said anything else for the rest of the trip home. As soon as the horse came to a stop in front of the barn, Amanda jumped out of the buggy and ran straight for the house. Not acknowledging her aunt, she raced upstairs to Bekah's bedroom, letting the tears she'd tried so hard to keep from falling slip down her cheeks. She threw herself facedown on the bed, resting her forehead on the crook of her elbow. "Sorry, *Daed*," she whispered, sniffing. "I'm not strong enough."

A knock sounded on the door, but she ignored it. When she heard Bekah calling her name, she didn't reply. If she pretended not to hear, maybe her cousin would go away. Several moments passed, and no one came into the room. Amanda closed her eyes. It had worked.

But no, the door opened. Bekah hadn't gotten the hint. Fine, it was her room. Amanda couldn't tell her to leave. But she didn't have to talk to her or even look at her. She didn't want to answer any more of her questions.

The bed moved as Bekah sat on it. Amanda felt a hand on her back, and she shrugged it off.

"Amanda."

She lifted her head in surprise. Instead of Bekah's face, she saw *Aenti* Margaret's. Her aunt's soft voice made her miss her mother even more. It also made more tears flow. Why couldn't she stop crying?

"Amanda, honey. Talk to me. You can't keep all of this inside."

She wiped her cheeks and sat up. While she could ignore Bekah, she couldn't avoid her aunt, not after the kindness she'd shown to her. "I'm fine. Don't worry about me."

"You're not fine." Her aunt's blue eyes were filled with concern. "You tried to run away. You could have been hurt, or worse." She tilted her head as she looked at Amanda. "There's something else too. You won't eat, and that's not healthy. You're going to get sick if you don't eat more often."

Amanda put her hands on the side of her head. "I just want to go home, *Aenti* Margaret. Please." She looked up at her aunt's face, meeting her eyes. "Can't you take me home?"

Pain crossed her aunt's face. "Amanda, *lieb*, I'd love that more than anything. Not because we don't want you here, because we do. But I know how much you miss your *daed*."

"I miss my *mutter* too."

"Of course you do." She wiped Amanda's damp cheek with the back of her hand. "I know you miss her. But right now your father's trying to convince her to come back home."

Amanda's eyes widened. "You know what happened to *Mamm*?"

"*Ya*. Your *daed* told us."

"But he said it was our secret! He made me promise not to say anything to you or *Onkel* Thomas. He didn't want me to say anything to anyone." Why could he talk about her mother, but she couldn't? New tears sprang to her eyes.

"Oh, sweetheart. He didn't have a choice. We needed to know what was going on so we could help you."

Amanda looked down at her lap. She understood why her father had to tell, but it didn't make her feel any better. Now they didn't even have that secret between them.

"Don't be upset with your *daed*. He's doing what he thinks is best for you. And he's trying very hard to help your *mami*. He can't do that and worry about you and take care of the farm. It's only for a little while, Amanda. You have to be strong—"

"But I can't! *Daed* told me the same thing, and I can't be strong. I hate it here." Guilt pressed at her as soon as she said the words, but she didn't care. She turned her back on her aunt again and crossed her arms, shutting her eyes tight as the tears fell down her face. "Please . . . just leave me alone."

Bekah leaned near the doorway of her room—as close as she dared. She shouldn't be listening in on her mother's conversation, but she had to find out what was going on with Amanda. Her father had been silent since they'd come back home, but the way his fists clenched and unclenched told her he was also upset. When they had returned from putting up Sparky, Bekah had run upstairs, hoping to catch her cousin, but her mother was already upstairs with her. Everything was so strange. She could hear snippets of the conversation, but she still had no idea what Amanda's problem was.

When she heard her mother's footsteps, Bekah jumped back and ran downstairs. She went into the kitchen and stood by the stove, pretending to stir the carrots, which were already cold, as her mother had turned off the stove while they were searching for Amanda. Her mother entered the kitchen the same time as her father came in the back door. They exchanged a look and left the room together. Bekah rolled her eyes. Everyone was having conversations that did not include her!

She crept to the kitchen door, hoping to find out something. Yes! They were in the living room. Perhaps if she held her breath, she could hear what her parents said.

"She won't come downstairs," her mother was saying.

"She's been through a lot," *Daed* said. "Give her time."

"I have. And I will. I just wish . . ."

"I know," *Daed* said in a low voice. "We all wish things were different."

"I don't like seeing her so sad. I'm not sure this is the best place for her, Thomas. Maybe she should have stayed in Paradise. She's miserable here. Bekah's been trying to make her feel at home here, but nothing she does seems to work."

Bekah couldn't help but smile a tiny bit. At least her mother knew she was trying her best with Amanda. That meant a lot.

"We can't take her back, Margaret. Not until Ezra says it's time. We gave him our word, remember?"

"I remember." Her mother sighed more loudly.

"Ezra wanted Amanda away from the situation. I don't blame him." Her father paused. "He didn't want her to deal with the repercussions of her mother's choice."

Bekah brought her hand to her mouth. *Choice? What choice?*

"But what if he can't convince Caroline to come back?" Her mother sounded upset.

"Then we'll keep Amanda as long as Ezra needs us to."

"She's welcome to stay here as long as she wants, but I still don't think it's *gut* for the two of them to be apart. They'll need each other if Caroline decides not to return."

"Listen to me, Margaret. We have to put this in God's hands. That's what Ezra said he was doing. He said God led him to ask us to keep Amanda. We prayed about it and thought it was God's will also. We never said this was going to be easy—on any of us, but especially on Amanda."

"I know." Bekah heard her mother walk across the room. She shrank back into the kitchen, breathing a sigh of relief when she wasn't discovered. Then *Mami* began to speak again. "I just don't understand what has gotten into Caroline. How could she leave her husband and *kinn*? What kind of mother decides that she doesn't want to be with her family anymore?"

Bekah's mind was reeling. *Aenti* Caroline had . . . run away? Who had ever heard of such a thing?

"Shh, Margaret. It's not our place to judge or gossip about her. Ezra wanted to keep that kind of talk away from Amanda. She doesn't need to hear it from us."

"You're right. I'm sorry." Her mother didn't speak for a moment, then continued. "We should at least tell Katherine and Bekah why Amanda's here. Bekah's already suspicious. She's been asking a lot of questions."

"That doesn't surprise me. She's always been curious." Her father let out a half-hearted chuckle. "But I don't know if we should say anything to the *maed*. Ezra asked us not to. I don't want to break my *bruder*'s trust in us."

Mami sighed. "*Ya*. I understand. But I don't like keeping things from our *kinner* either."

Bekah bit her bottom lip. Ever since Amanda had arrived, she knew her parents had been keeping something from her. Yet from what she could gather, they had good reason to. And now she was more curious than ever about what was going on with her aunt and why she left. No wonder Amanda was acting so strangely and seemed so sad. Even though Bekah didn't know the whole story, and she wouldn't if her uncle got his way, this was enough to understand why her mother didn't want her giving up on Amanda. And now she felt more guilty than ever for yelling at her earlier.

When she heard her parents coming toward her, she went to the stove and pretended to stir the carrots again. What she really wanted to do was go upstairs and see Amanda. But she couldn't let her parents know she had heard their conversation.

Her mother came up behind her. "Bekah, will you *geh* upstairs and tell Amanda supper is ready? We're going to try this again."

Bekah nodded, glad for the chance to see her cousin. She hurried upstairs, then stopped at the door, taking a moment to collect herself. She had a million questions, but how could she ask them without making Amanda suspicious? Then again, she should probably mind her own business. That's what her mother would tell her to do. She didn't know what choice to make, but she couldn't wait outside the room much longer; her mother would be expecting them both to come downstairs. She knocked on the door, determined to tell Amanda about supper and nothing more.

When Amanda didn't respond, Bekah knocked again. Silence. Bekah slowly opened the door and walked inside. Amanda was lying on the bed, facing the wall. Her face was buried in the white afghan. Bekah went over and nudged her on the shoulder. "Amanda?"

Amanda didn't say anything, and Bekah watched her for a moment. From the rhythmic rise and fall of her cousin's chest she could see Amanda had fallen asleep, and Bekah backed away from the bed, not wanting to wake her.

She was about to turn around when she heard the sound of a car pulling into the driveway next door. She looked outside, her eyes widening with surprise. The old man was back! Forgetting her promise not to be nosy, she moved closer to the window and watched. He opened the van door and stepped outside. Then he went to the back of the van and flipped open the back hatch. He pulled out a large chest, which looked like it opened from the top and had several handles and hinges all over it. He set it on the ground and shut the door again, then picked up the chest. She expected him to go inside through the front of the house, but instead he took the chest with him and went to the back, just as he'd done a few days before.

Supper slipping from her mind, Bekah leaned out the window, trying to get a better view of him, but he had disappeared. She frowned, confused. Why would he go through the back door instead of the front? She knew he had a key, so why not use it? Especially when he was carrying that chest? It looked heavy. Wouldn't it be easier to go through the front door?

Suddenly she remembered what her mother had said about minding her own business, and sighed. She'd never figure out what was going on next door. She withdrew from the window and went downstairs, glancing at Amanda one last time to make sure she was still asleep before she left the bedroom.

When Bekah reached the kitchen, her mother had already filled Bekah's plate with food. She looked at Bekah and frowned. "Where is Amanda?"

"She's sleeping. I didn't want to wake her up."

Her mother nodded, but Bekah didn't miss the sadness in her eyes. "That's probably for the best. We'll save her a plate for later."

Bekah and her parents ate the meal in silence. She was dying to ask them about Amanda's mother, but she couldn't. How was she going to find out what happened if no one would talk to her?

After they finished eating, Bekah helped her mother clean the kitchen. *Mami* saved a generous portion of the chicken and rice casserole for Amanda, then made a second plate for Katherine. She wrapped both in foil and left them on the counter. When the kitchen was finished, Bekah's mother went to the living room, where her father was already reading the paper. As she often did in the evenings, *Mami* would work on her sewing until bedtime.

Bekah looked at the kitchen clock: almost half-past eight. Katherine would be home soon, so she decided to wait on her sister. Maybe Katherine knew something about Amanda's mother. She got a book from the shelf in the living room, then went back in the kitchen to read until Katherine arrived.

Fifteen minutes later Katherine walked into the kitchen.

"I'm so glad the day is over." Katherine plopped down at the table, setting her purse on top of it. She bent over and slipped off her black shoes, then sat up and let out a long, weary-sounding sigh. "We were busy from the first moment of my shift until it ended. It seemed like everyone in Middlefield came into the restaurant tonight." She looked at the two plates on the counter and smiled. "Oh, *danki* for saving me dinner. I didn't get a chance to eat, we were so swamped." She stood and crossed the room, lifting the foil on the plate. "Who's this one for?" she said, pointing to the covered dish beside it.

Bekah put down her book. "That's for Amanda."

Katherine opened the silverware drawer and pulled out a fork. She carried her plate to the table and pulled the foil back all the way. "Mmm, it looks good. It's still a little warm."

"We ate late tonight."

Katherine bowed her head and prayed, then picked up her fork. "So why didn't Amanda eat at suppertime?"

Frowning, Bekah said, "Because she left."

"Left? What do you mean?"

Bekah explained about Amanda running away and how she and her father had to go get her and bring her back. "Then she went upstairs and fell asleep," Bekah said, finishing the story. "*Mami* had fixed her favorite meal for her, so she saved her a plate for later, in case she was hungry." Bekah glanced at the foil-covered dish.

Katherine stuck the tine of her fork in one of the carrots. "I can't believe she ran away. Why would she do something like that?"

Bekah shrugged. Knowing her parents were in the next room and could come in at any moment, she leaned closer to Katherine. "Can I talk to you later? Privately?"

Her left brow raising, Katherine nodded. "*Ya*. I'll meet you in my room as soon as I'm finished here."

Bekah nodded. She picked up her book and headed upstairs. As she passed by the living room, her mother called out her name. Bekah stepped inside the room. "*Ya*?"

Mami got up from the couch and walked over to her. She drew Bekah into a tight hug. "Just wanted to tell you *guten nacht, lieb.*"

Bekah leaned into her mother's hug, thinking about Amanda and her mother. *I have to figure out a way to help her. I just wish I knew how.*

Eight

Bekah paced in her sister's room upstairs, waiting on Katherine. It sure seemed like she was taking her own sweet time. As she walked through the door, Bekah started in. "Did you know *Aenti* Caroline left *Onkel* Ezra?"

Katherine closed the door behind her. "Shhh. You want Amanda to hear?"

Bekah shook her head as Katherine sat on the bed. Bekah bounced down beside her. "Well?" she asked. "Did you know?"

Katherine nodded. "*Ya*. I did know."

Bekah jumped up from the bed. "What? Why did *Mami* and *Daed* tell you, but not me?" Hurt coursed through her. They trusted Katherine more than her?

"Don't be upset, Bekah. They didn't tell me. Right before Amanda came, I needed the buggy to *geh* to town. As I got near the barn I could hear *Daed* on the cell phone. He was talking to *Onkel* Ezra. That's the only reason I know."

Bekah took a deep breath. She walked over to the bed and sat down next to Katherine again, glad her parents hadn't left her out. She was also glad she wasn't the only person eavesdropping. "That's why Amanda ran away today," she told Katherine. "She wanted to go back home to her *daed*."

"I don't blame her." Katherine looked down at her lap and smoothed out a wrinkle in the skirt of her light blue dress. Then she looked at Bekah, her blue eyes filled with confusion. "I can't believe *Aenti* Caroline would do something like this. And poor Amanda." Katherine shook her head. "I feel so bad for her."

"Me too. But I don't know what to do to help her feel better. She won't talk to me or do anything."

Katherine gave her a small smile. "I know. I wish I could do something to help her too. I've been working so much lately that I haven't spent any time with her." She paused. "But I have a couple of days off next week. Maybe I can do something with her then. I could teach her how to crochet."

"That's a great idea. She sleeps with that white afghan you made me for Christmas last year."

"She does?" Katherine looked pleased. "All right. That's something we can do together. I'll make sure to suggest it to her on my next day off."

Bekah nodded, feeling a little better that she didn't have the sole responsibility for Amanda. "Do you think we should ask *Mami* and *Daed* about *Aenti* Caroline?"

Katherine shrugged. "I don't know. I wonder why they haven't told us about it yet?"

"Because *Onkel* Ezra doesn't want them to. *Daed* said he gave him his word."

"Then I don't think we should ask him to break it, do you?"

"*Nee*." Bekah bit the inside of both lips, shaking her head. "Katherine, why do you think she left?"

"I have no idea. But I'm going to pray she comes back to *Onkel* Ezra, and soon."

"Me too."

Bekah smiled at her sister. They hadn't talked like this in a long time, and even though she was still concerned about Amanda, she was glad to spend a little time with Katherine. She rarely saw her anymore—she doubted Katherine even knew about the old man next door. "Did you know someone has moved into the Harpers' place? At least I think he's moved in."

Katherine looked surprised. "What do you mean, you think so?"

"Well, I'm not sure. He's come over a couple of times. He has a key, and I just saw him take a big trunk to the backyard earlier today." Bekah didn't think her sister needed to know about the other man who had been over there. She definitely didn't want to discuss him.

"So you've met him?"

Bekah shook her head. "*Nee*."

"Then how did you see him take the trunk to the backyard?" She looked genuinely confused for a moment, then nodded. "You were peeking out the window in your room, right?"

"Only for a little bit." Bekah steeled herself for another warning about how she shouldn't be so nosy, but Katherine didn't mention it.

"I was kind of hoping a family would move in." Katherine got up from the bed and walked over to her dresser. She started to take the bobby pins out of her *kapp*, placing them on top of the dresser.

"Me too. But maybe he's nice. Or has some nice grandchildren who will come visit."

Katherine took off her *kapp* and yawned. "Maybe."

She looks tired, Bekah thought. She told her sister good night and went back to her room.

She crept inside, removed the clips holding her kerchief in place, and slipped into her nightgown. She started for her bed, then glanced at the window. She wasn't going to spy—but she couldn't resist just a quick peek. Lights were on inside. Then Bekah saw the thin beam of a flashlight in the backyard. She froze, peering more closely. The man came out of the back of the house, carrying his flashlight and something else she couldn't see. He traveled to the back edge of the yard and put the flashlight down on the ground.

What is he doing? Bekah tried to see, but she had a hard time making out his movements. Then she realized what he had in his hands. A shovel. He started to dig a hole in his backyard. Which itself wasn't strange—but why not wait until morning when there was plenty of light? At least he could see what he was doing then.

Fascinated, Bekah watched as he dug the hole, suddenly

stopping and picking up the flashlight. He reached into one of the pockets of his trousers and pulled something out of it. She couldn't tell what it was, but a flash of movement caught her eye as he dropped the object into the hole. Then he put the flashlight back on the ground, filled in the hole with dirt, and went back into the house.

She watched to see if he would come back out. Five minutes passed and nothing happened, so she went to bed, still puzzling over the man digging in the backyard. As soon as she slid under the covers, Amanda turned over. Bekah wondered if she had been awake the whole time.

"Amanda?"

"What?"

Her cousin didn't sound sleepy at all. *I bet she was awake*, Bekah thought. She knew she had to be careful with what she said to Amanda from now on. "There's a plate of food downstairs for you to eat if you're hungry. I know it's late, but I don't think *Mami* will mind if you want to eat."

Amanda didn't answer right away. Finally she said, "I don't want anything." Then she paused for a long time. "*Danki*, though."

"You're welcome." Bekah lay there, feeling like she should say something else. She knew about Amanda's mother, and she felt sorry about it. But she wasn't sure what she could say. Finally she said, "If you, um, need to talk about something, let me know. Okay?"

Amanda rolled over, putting her back to Bekah. "*Guten nacht.*"

Bekah sighed. *Lord, help my cousin. And my aunt and uncle. Please bring their family back together. If anyone can do it, you can.*

Sunday, after church service, Bekah walked over to the swing and sat down, still thinking about her parents' conversation from earlier in the week. She wished Amanda would talk to her, but now she knew trying to get answers out of her cousin would be impossible. Bekah had tried all week, but Amanda was more tight-lipped than her parents! Bekah didn't say anything about *Aenti* Caroline, and she tried to come up with things for them to do so Amanda wouldn't think about home. But after the day she tried to run away, Amanda withdrew further into herself. She still ate very little food, even though Bekah's mother made her favorite meals. Even Katherine had tried, first by offering to show her how to crochet, then by suggesting they go to Middlefield for an ice cream sundae at Mary Yoder's. But Amanda had refused, just as she refused Bekah's offer to play outside, or practice sewing, or take a walk down the road to see the Troyers' cows. Most of the time Amanda wanted to stay in the bedroom and be alone. Bekah didn't know what to do, and from the daily strain she saw on her mother's face, Bekah knew she wasn't the only one struggling.

Fortunately, members of the school board had passed the word through the district that the repairs were finished and school could finally open on Monday. Bekah had been relieved to hear the news—she was more ready for school than ever before. She had mentioned it to Amanda earlier that day, hoping to drum up some enthusiasm.

"I'm excited about school." Bekah buttered a thick piece of homemade bread before putting a slice of trail bologna on it. They were making a light supper after the bounty of Sunday lunch. "Aren't you?" It didn't surprise her when Amanda shook her head. But Bekah still tried. "You'll like our teacher, *Fraulein* Byler. She was at church this morning. She was sitting two rows in front of us."

"I didn't see her." Amanda picked up a slice of Swiss cheese and put it on her plate. She added a piece of bread and started for the kitchen table.

"Is that all you want for supper? We've got pickles and potato chips too."

Amanda shook her head and went to the table, where Katherine and her parents were already seated. Bekah met her sister's gaze, then shrugged. If Amanda didn't want to eat much, Bekah wouldn't worry about it. Frankly, she was tired of trying to be happy around Amanda all the time. It was exhausting, and didn't seem to do much good anyway. Amanda continued to mope, but Bekah went outside after the meal.

With a sigh, she dug her toe in the dirt and pushed, moving the swing back and forth. She had been so excited when she first heard about Amanda coming to visit. Now she and the rest of her family were miserable.

She glanced up and saw the Harpers' house. The minivan wasn't in the driveway, and Bekah hadn't seen the old man since that night he had been digging in his backyard. But she'd been so consumed with Amanda that she hadn't paid much attention to what was going on next door.

Before Bekah and Amanda went to bed that night, *Mami* knocked on the bedroom door. She opened it and walked in, smiling. "I brought a few things for Amanda." She held up a light blue dress, the one Bekah had seen her working on earlier in the week, then handed it to Amanda. "I thought you'd like something new to start the first day of school."

Amanda took the dress and draped it over her arm. "*Danki*. I'll wear it tomorrow."

Mami's smile slipped at Amanda's reaction, and Bekah didn't blame her. Her cousin could have been more grateful. After all, she had shown up with one dress—a torn one at that—while *Mami* had taken the time to alter one of Katherine's to make her a new one.

"I also brought you something else." *Mami* held out a white plastic bag. "Brand-new school supplies for tomorrow."

Amanda took the bag and nodded. She placed it on the floor next to the dresser.

Mami waited for a moment, her lips pressing together. Then she walked over to the window and pulled the white curtains closed. "It's getting close to bedtime. Make sure you say your prayers." She smiled at them both, but only Bekah smiled back.

After her mother had left, Bekah and Amanda knelt down at the edge of their bed and they both said their silent prayers. Bekah closed her eyes.

Dear Lord, I pray for a gut *day at school tomorrow, and that you'll be with* Fraulein *Byler, our new teacher. I also pray that Caleb sits far away from me and won't bug me too much this year. And please, Lord, cheer up Amanda, because we can't.*

She heard a rustling movement next to her and opened one eye. Amanda was already finished with her prayers and had climbed into bed. Bekah noticed that Amanda's prayers were becoming shorter every night. Bekah closed her eyes and continued to pray.

Help her to find friends so she can be happier. I know she misses her home, but I hope someday she won't mind being here too much. Amen.

Bekah opened her eyes and slung her long ponytail over her shoulder before climbing into bed. There was a bit of fading light still peeking in underneath the curtain. She stared at the ceiling, too antsy to sleep. She turned her head to the side. "Amanda? Are you still awake?"

Amanda had her back to her and didn't respond. Bekah had never met anyone who could fall asleep so fast. Letting out a deep breath, she rolled over on her side and closed her eyes. She started mentally counting the cows in the Troyers' herd. That usually bored her to sleep. But she was only on number five when she saw car lights illuminate the window. She sat up on her right elbow and listened. The window was open, and she could hear the sound of the car's engine. Then it stopped, and the lights went out. The old man must have come back.

She pressed her teeth against her lip, fighting the urge

to go to the window, remembering what her mother had told her about minding her own business. But after a few minutes, her curiosity won, and she slipped out of bed and crept to the window, careful not to disturb Amanda. Bekah slowly pulled back the white curtain, just enough so she could peek out but not be seen. Her eyes widened when she saw the minivan in the driveway. Even though it was nearly nightfall, she recognized it. She watched as the old man got out, but instead of going straight inside, he opened up the back trunk of the van and pulled out two large suitcases. He stopped in front of the door and put the suitcases down on the concrete landing. There was still enough light left that she could see him fumble for his key. He opened the front door and went inside. A few moments later a light went on in the house.

Bekah settled against the window ledge. What she wouldn't do for a chance to peek inside the house. Everything about the man was so odd. Last time he was here he had that trunk. Now he had suitcases. But she had yet to see a moving truck. Had he bought the house or not?

It occurred to her that she should go downstairs and tell her parents about this, but she decided not to. It could wait until morning. Besides, her mother would not only scold her for spying, but also for not going right to sleep after she had told them good night.

She shifted her body to get a better view of the house and waited to see if the old man came back outside. After about ten minutes, the last pale sliver of sunlight disappeared, but he didn't show. Soon after, the light turned out. Bekah waited a couple of minutes more, then gave up and went back to bed.

She tossed and turned on the bed, trying to get to sleep. Amanda didn't stir, and Bekah was glad her cousin was a sound sleeper. Bekah groaned and flopped on her stomach. She had to get up early in the morning to get ready for school, and she didn't want to be sleepy on her first day. But she couldn't stop thinking about the old man. She didn't have a good feeling about him, but at least she wasn't afraid of him—not like she was afraid of the man with the tattoos. She didn't know what she'd do if he ever showed up again.

Nine

MONDAY MORNING, despite the lack of sleep, Bekah woke up early. Before she got out of bed she glanced at Amanda, who was still asleep facing the wall. She made a little more noise than usual getting ready, hoping Amanda would take the hint and get up. But Amanda didn't move. After putting on her black stockings, she leaned over and nudged Amanda. "Wake up. Time to get ready for school."

Amanda slowly rolled over. She flung her arm over her eyes as Bekah opened the curtains to let in the morning sunlight. "Already?"

"*Ya. Mami* always makes chocolate chip pancakes and sausage for the first day of school." She sniffed. "I can already smell them. I'm going downstairs and get them while they're hot."

Amanda nodded, but she remained still. Bekah scowled. She didn't want to deal with her cousin's moodiness this morning. The first day of school was one of her favorite days of the year, and she wasn't going to let anyone spoil it. She shrugged and flew downstairs, feeling the strings of her black *kapp* sailing behind her. When she ran into the kitchen, the delicious smell of breakfast hit her full force. Oh, how she loved the first day of school! "Mmmmm," she said, standing next to her mother.

Mami had just poured a scoopful of pancake batter on the hot frying pan. Lots of small dark spots dotted the white batter. Bekah smiled. Her mother had added extra chocolate chips. She watched as the batter bubbled and solidified at the edges. "Can I flip them?"

Her mother nodded and handed Bekah the spatula. Bekah carefully slid the spatula underneath the pancake and turned it over. A little of the batter splashed, but that didn't matter. The other side was a perfect golden brown.

"Is Amanda up?" *Mami* asked. She poured orange juice into the glasses on the table.

"I woke her up before I came down." Bekah kept her eye on the pancakes, not wanting to burn them. There were few things worse than burned chocolate chip pancakes. In another fry pan, next to the pancakes, were thick patties of pork sausage. The fat snapped and sizzled in the pan. Bekah's stomach growled.

"I think the sausage is done. There's a plate next to the stove. Could you put the patties on it, please? I'm going to *geh* upstairs and check on Amanda."

"Where's Katherine?"

"She spent the night with Mary Beth. They're both working early this morning, and Johnny offered to take them to Mary Yoder's on his way to work."

"I'm sure Katherine will love that," Bekah mumbled.

"What's that?"

"*Nix.*" Bekah had no idea if her mother knew about Katherine's crush on Johnny, even though her sister wasn't subtle about it. Still, it wasn't Bekah's job to tell her mother about it. She could keep a secret, even if her parents didn't think so. She put the sausage on the plate and finished off the pancakes.

A few moments later her mother and Amanda came downstairs. Amanda had on the dress *Mami* had given to her last night. It looked nice on her, but Amanda didn't seem happy to be wearing it.

Her father came inside from taking care of Sparky, and they all sat down to eat. They all bowed their heads for silent prayer. Afterward, *Daed* reached for the pancakes. Bekah suddenly remembered about the old man next door. She was just about to open her mouth when her father spoke. "I see we have a new neighbor. Just saw him outside this morning."

"Did you talk to him?" *Mami* asked, taking a slice of sausage and putting it on her plate.

"Not really. He told me he moved in last night, but he didn't say much else. Doesn't seem too friendly."

Bekah hid a frown. She could have told her father that. The old man looked anything but friendly. She took the plate of pancakes from her father and put three of them on her dish.

"So the Harpers' house finally sold." Her mother smiled. "I'm glad for them. It's been for sale for a long time."

Her father held up his hand. "I'm not sure it sold, Margaret. He could be renting it for all we know. He wasn't forthcoming about anything, that's for sure. When I went over to introduce myself, he was standing by his van. He had the engine running and seemed to be in a hurry." He looked at Bekah, then at Amanda. "I still don't want you going over there. Not until I get to know him better."

Bekah and Amanda both nodded. Her father didn't have to worry. Even though she wanted to know what was going on, Bekah had no plans to go next door. It didn't take long to eat the breakfast, and after they were done her mother handed both her and Amanda their lunch boxes. "Have a *gut* day," she said, ushering them out the door. Amanda walked out first. *Mami* put her hand on Bekah's shoulder. "Make sure you help your cousin today."

Bekah stifled a sigh. She hoped Amanda would try to be more cheerful at school than she was at home, but Bekah doubted it. "I will, *Mami*."

Mami squeezed her shoulder and smiled. "*Danki*, Bekah. I appreciate it."

Bolstered by her mother's words, Bekah skipped to catch up with Amanda, who was already halfway down the road. The schoolhouse was about two miles away from their house. She glanced at the Harpers' house as she passed. Of course, she couldn't call it that anymore, now that someone else was living there. Putting the old man and the house out of her mind, she fell in step beside Amanda.

The morning was already hot, and perspiration broke out on Bekah's forehead as they turned left and walked along the side of the road. But as the schoolhouse came into view, Amanda slowed her pace. Bekah was five steps ahead of her when she noticed. "We're gonna be late if you don't hurry up, Amanda," she said over her shoulder. "I don't think *Fraulein* Byler will appreciate that."

The warning spurred Amanda on, and she walked a little faster, catching up to Bekah.

When she was younger, Bekah used to run the last few yards to school, and a part of her wanted to do that now. But she was thirteen years old, and while she was just as excited on the first day of school as she always was, she was in seventh grade and one of the oldest students in the school. She needed to act accordingly. But the urge to dash to the playground was tempting.

When they arrived at the *schulhaus*, several children were already outside on the small playground next to the building. The green grass had been cut short, and a volleyball net was set up in the back corner. A large oak tree was situated a few feet away from it, its long branches and dense leaves forming a perfect canopy of shade. Bekah found her friends, Ester and Miriam, standing under it, and she walked over to them.

"Guten morgen," she said to her friends as she neared. They waved at her in greeting.

"Who is your friend?" Miriam asked. She was a petite girl with black hair and large blue eyes.

"My cousin Amanda. She's from Pennsylvania, but she's staying with us for a little while. Amanda, this is—" Bekah turned to introduce her cousin to Miriam when she saw Amanda was walking toward the school. When she got to the building, she leaned against it, holding her lunch box against her thin chest.

Great. Bekah tried not to show her exasperation. She didn't want to walk across the playground to get her cousin. She wanted to spend time with Miriam and Ester. She hadn't seen them for a while—Ester had missed church last Sunday, and Miriam had spent a couple of weeks visiting family in Sarasota, Florida.

Ester stepped forward, tilting her head to the left as she looked at Amanda. "Why is she standing over there by herself?" Unlike Miriam, Ester was tall and stocky, with full cheeks and light hazel eyes. They were opposites, and the best of friends.

"She's shy." Bekah hoped she wouldn't have to make excuses for her cousin for the rest of the year. But she couldn't explain what was really going on with Amanda, not when she didn't even understand it herself. Shrugging, she turned to her friends. "It'll take some time for her to come around." *I hope*. "But once she does, you'll really like her."

"It must be hard being the new *maedel* in *schul*," Ester said. "Is she in our grade?"

"*Nee*, she's in sixth."

"Well, I'll make sure to sit next to her this morning," Ester said. "I'm sure *Fraulein* Byler will put us in assigned seats, but until then I'll do what I can to make her feel welcome."

Bekah smiled. Ester was the nicest girl she knew, and Bekah appreciated someone helping her with Amanda. Maybe Amanda would open up to Ester.

"Oh, there's Caleb." Miriam pointed in the direction of the volleyball net.

Bekah glanced at him. He was standing by the net with his friend Melvin, who had the bad luck of being the shortest boy in the class. Caleb could easily prop his elbow on top of Melvin's head without having to bend or hunch. Melvin wore his straw hat tipped back, and he was laughing at something Caleb said. Suddenly Caleb turned, his gaze landing on Bekah. For some weird reason her cheeks felt hot, and she looked away. *Must be the heat.*

"I wonder who that new *bu* is?" Ester said. For the first time, Bekah noticed another boy standing near Caleb and Melvin. He was taller than Caleb and looked older. Caleb was tossing the volleyball up and down in his right hand. Then he gestured with his head toward the volleyball net. The boy shook his head. Caleb and Melvin looked at each other for a moment, then started up a volleyball game with a couple other boys. "I've never seen him before," Bekah said.

"It's been a long time since we've had new students in school," Ester said, still watching the boy. "Now we have two."

"Who cares about him?" Miriam craned her neck to see past Bekah. "I'd rather look at Caleb."

Bekah's eyes widened. "What?"

"Caleb." Miriam let out a breath, and Bekah frowned. Her friend sounded like Katherine did when she talked about Johnny. That wasn't a good thing. "Oh, *nee*. Don't tell me you like him, Miriam."

"What's not to like? He's funny. And cute. C'mon, Bekah. Even you have to admit that."

"*Nee*, I don't, because it's not true." But Bekah couldn't help but look at Caleb again. Funny? Cute? Had Miriam lost her mind? She couldn't imagine her friend really liking him. Just thinking about it made her stomach turn.

Ester swatted her hand at the air. "You might as well give up on him, Miriam. We all know there's only one *maedel* he has his eyes on."

"Who?" The question flew out of Bekah's mouth faster than she had intended it to. "Not that I care or anything."

Ester and Miriam looked at each other and started laughing.

"What?" Bekah asked, bewildered.

Fraulein Byler called the students to come in. Her friends laughed again and dashed to the *schulhaus*, not answering Bekah's question. Fine, she didn't care who Caleb Mullet liked. As long as it wasn't her. Or Miriam. Or Ester. But that was because she cared about her friends, and she wouldn't want them to have to put up with him. That was the only reason.

They piled into the school and filed into seats. True to her word, Ester sought out Amanda and sat next to her.

Bekah was glad when she saw Amanda give Ester a small smile.

But a few minutes later the seating had changed. *Fraulein* Byler moved the younger children to the front and the older ones to the back. Because several desks had been destroyed in the accident, there was a long table in the back of the room to take the place of the desks, and *Fraulein* Byler directed the older students to sit at it. "It's just temporary," she said. "We should have new desks soon."

Bekah, Ester, and Miriam moved to the back of the room and sat in the chairs behind the table. They were the only seventh grade girls. Caleb, Melvin, and a couple of eighth graders, including the new boy, sat farther down.

Bekah could see Amanda sitting at a desk two rows in front of her. In front of every student there was a brand-new spiral notebook and pencil. Bekah sat down and looked at her red notebook. Her name was written in the upper-right-hand corner.

Fraulein Byler clapped her hands. "Now, I want everyone to find your seats please. *Danki.*" Once everyone was seated, she closed her eyes for a brief moment. Bekah thought her teacher must be praying.

She opened her eyes and walked to the blackboard behind the desk. "*Guten morgen, kinner.*" She held her arm up, an uncertain expression on her face. Bekah could see she was nervous.

Fraulein Byler introduced herself by writing her name on the blackboard. After her introduction she said, "And we're going to have a great time learning to be *gut* and diligent students."

Lori Fisher raised her tiny hand. The tow-headed girl was the youngest student in the class, barely six. "What does *dilibent* mean?"

"Not dilibent. *Diligent*. Diligent means to take *gut* care of your work. To do it to the best of your ability, thoroughly, and turn it in on time."

"And what if we don't?"

Bekah leaned forward and looked down the table to see who had spoken. She realized it was the new boy she and her friends had noticed on the playground before school began. The boys had taken their hats off when they came into the school, hanging them on a brand-new row of pegs in the back of the classroom, so she got a good look at his face. He had dark brown hair and thick eyebrows that almost met in the middle of his brow bone. He was slouching in his chair, his arms crossed over his chest, a sullen expression on his face.

"What if we don't what?" *Fraulein* Byler asked him. She looked startled by his question.

"Be diligent. What happens if we aren't?"

"Well . . ." She grabbed a pair of silver-framed glasses and put them on, then picked up a notebook with a dark green cover. "Jacob." She looked at him, peering at him over her glasses. "If you're not diligent, you'll have to face the consequences."

"What consequences?"

"I was just about to explain those to all of you."

Bekah leaned her chin in her hand as she listened to *Fraulein* Byler go over the class rules—rules she'd heard every year since she started school. As *Fraulein* Byler continued to speak, she seemed to become more relaxed. Bekah was glad. Her teacher was a year older than Katherine, but since they went to church together, Bekah had known her for a long time. She liked her and wanted her to do well.

The scent of fresh paint filtered throughout the one-room schoolhouse as Bekah continued to glance around the room. Once again her gaze landed on Jacob, who was still slouched in his seat in front of the long table. His posture reminded her of Amanda, only instead of looking sad he looked angry, like he didn't want to be in school. Then he put his head down, resting it on his forearms. His bending over gave her full view of Caleb—who turned and gave her his familiar smirk.

Bekah immediately turned back around and faced the front. Why did he always seem to know when she was looking at him?

"Jacob, I would appreciate it if you would give me your attention while I'm talking," *Fraulein* Byler said, interrupting Bekah's thoughts. Bekah glanced at her teacher, then looked at Jacob again. His head was still down.

"I'm paying attention," he said, his voice muffled. He didn't move.

"It doesn't look that way to me," *Fraulein* Byler said. "When you're paying attention to someone, you're looking directly at them."

Jacob lifted his head and stared at her, almost mocking. "Better?" he asked, his tone as disrespectful as his expression.

Bekah was stunned. She'd never seen a boy act out like this in school. The whole class seemed to feel the same way. No one said a single word.

Fraulein Byler didn't answer right away. Bekah could tell she was surprised by Jacob's behavior too. "*Ya*," she finally said slowly. "*Danki*."

Jacob tilted his head to the side and continued to stare at the teacher. Bekah shifted uncomfortably in her chair. The entire class was silent. Even Caleb, who was sitting right next to him, looked unnerved.

But *Fraulein* Byler didn't give Jacob any more attention. Instead, she walked over to a tall bookshelf stuffed with books. For the next half hour she handed out textbooks, even to Jacob, who remained quiet throughout the process and accepted his books without argument. Bekah breathed a sigh of relief. Finally, it seemed like a normal school day.

"I'd like you to spend the next several minutes writing about your summer break," *Fraulein* Byler said once she'd handed out all the books. She went to the blackboard and picked up a piece of white chalk. "I'd like you to write this heading at the top of the page: your name, today's date, Writing Assignment 1."

Bekah opened her journal and followed the directions. Then she heard the sound of something hitting the floor. Her head jerked up.

Fraulein Byler spun around. "What was that?"

Billy raised his hand. "Jacob shoved his notebook on the floor."

The teacher frowned, making her look like she had just sucked on a lemon. "Jacob, please pick up your journal and start your writing assignment."

He looked at her for a moment, then stomped his foot on top of the journal. "Oops." Sarcasm dripped from the word. But he didn't pick up the notebook.

Fraulein Byler looked at him, her lips tugging into an even deeper frown. "*Kinner*, please start on your assignments. Jacob, I'd like to see you outside for a moment."

Jacob sauntered to the front of the room, then out the door with *Fraulein* Byler following behind him. The students left behind barely seemed to breathe, it was so quiet. A few minutes passed before Bekah heard the teacher calling out for Jacob. She wished she were near a window so she could see what was going on. Caleb had popped up out of his seat and stood near the door. Bekah scowled at him. "What do you think you're doing?" she said in a loud whisper.

"Finding out what's going on." He held up his hand. "So be quiet!"

Bekah shook her head. One day his nosiness would get him into real trouble. She just hoped she wouldn't be around when it did.

Suddenly he scrambled back to his seat—and sat down just as *Fraulein* Byler walked inside. Jacob wasn't with her, and after a few minutes it was clear he had left. She looked tired, and again Bekah felt a little sorry for her. First school started a week late, and now a student actually left school without permission. Her poor teacher was having a hard time of it.

Ten

A COUPLE of hours later *Fraulein* Byler dismissed them for lunch and recess. Bekah took her lunch box from underneath her bench. Since it was a nice day, the teacher let them eat outside, and Bekah and her friends went to sit underneath the oak tree with a few of their classmates.

When Bekah sat down, she opened her lunch box and saw what her mother had packed—a peanut butter and jelly sandwich, an oatmeal raisin cookie, and an apple. Her stomach growled. She bowed her head and said a quick, silent prayer, then picked up her sandwich.

"Your cousin's eating by herself." Ester took a bite of her sandwich and tilted her head in the direction of the schoolhouse.

Bekah bit her lip and turned around. In all the excitement of the morning she'd forgotten about Amanda. Her cousin wasn't even sitting down; she was leaning against the building much the same way she had done that morning. Bekah set down her lunch box. "I'll be right back," she said to her friends, then crossed the playground to get Amanda.

When she reached her cousin, Bekah stopped in front of her. "Come sit with us under the tree, Amanda. It's a lot cooler there, and I'll introduce you to my friends. You already met Ester, but Miriam would like to meet you too."

Amanda looked hesitant, and Bekah thought she'd have to drag her across the playground, but to her surprise Amanda agreed. As they walked back toward the tree, a baseball plunked Bekah in the leg. "Ow!" A sharp pain ran through her shin and calf. She knelt down on the ground, and Amanda crouched beside her.

Caleb, along with three of his friends, ran up to her. "Sorry," he said.

She looked up at him, ready to yell, but she stopped when she saw the look on his face. His mouth tilted into a frown, and he looked more serious than she'd ever seen him. Maybe he was really sorry.

The boys had left their hats inside, and Caleb shoved a hand through his hair. "Bekah, I didn't do it on purpose, I promise. Melvin threw a curve ball, and I tipped it off the top of the bat."

"He did," Melvin said. His four front teeth pressed against his top lip, showing his huge overbite. "I always throw pitches he can't handle."

"*Nee*, you don't. That was a fluke."

"Then what do you call your last three turns at bat?" Melvin grinned. "Strikeouts, that's what."

Bekah tuned out their argument and looked at her leg. The ball had bounced off her calf muscle, clipping part of her shin too. While it stung, it didn't hurt too much right now. She'd probably have a big bruise later. "Don't worry about it. I'm okay."

Caleb breathed out a sigh. "*Gut*. I didn't want you whining to *Fraulein* about getting hit."

She groaned and glared at him. Just when she was starting to think he might be a decent person, he proved her wrong again. "*Geh* back to your *dumm* game." She should have known he didn't feel bad for hitting her. That would be too much to ask. Caleb Mullet would never change.

The boys dashed to the other side of the play yard and continued their game.

"Are you okay?"

Bekah looked at Amanda, who was still kneeling beside her. "*Ya*, I'm fine. Just hurts a little bit." Bekah stood up and limped back to the tree.

"I don't think he meant to hit you."

Bekah grimaced. Why did everyone defend him? "Oh, he meant to. You don't know him as well as I do."

"He looked really sorry."

"It's an act. Trust me." Bekah got to her feet, wincing at the ache in her shin. "Caleb's never sorry for anything he does to me."

Amanda didn't say anything to that, and she and Bekah walked over to the tree to join Ester and Miriam, Bekah limping a little bit. She sat down by her lunch box, and Amanda sat between her and Ester. Bekah stretched her legs out in front of her.

"Wow." Ester glanced at Bekah's shin. "Caleb hit that ball pretty hard. That looked like it hurt."

"It did." She looked at her half-eaten peanut butter and jelly sandwich, suddenly losing her appetite. She shut the lid to the box.

"Caleb looked pretty worried." Miriam sighed, getting that same annoying dreamy look Katherine always got when she talked about Johnny. "He's cute when he's upset."

Bekah's stomach turned. What was it with the Mullet brothers? First her sister and Johnny, and now Miriam wasn't even trying to hide how much she liked Caleb. "Look, I don't want to talk about Caleb, okay?"

Ester and Miriam looked at each other. "We can change the subject if you want, Bekah."

Bekah nodded, tucking her legs underneath her dress, trying not to wince.

Then Miriam spoke. "What do you think about that *bu* walking out of the *schulhaus* this morning?"

"I can't believe he did that," Ester said, her eyes widening.

"I bet he'll be in big trouble with his parents when he gets home." Miriam nibbled on a carrot stick. "I know I would be if I did something like that."

"So would I," Bekah said. She looked at her cousin, expecting her to chime in.

But Amanda didn't respond at all. She kept her focus on her sandwich, taking tiny bites.

A few moments of silence passed. Bekah shifted as the awkwardness grew between the four girls. Finally, Ester turned to Amanda, giving her a tentative smile.

"So, Amanda. Have you been to Middlefield before?"

Amanda nibbled on the corner of her sandwich. "*Nee*. This is my first time."

"We always visited Amanda and her family in Paradise," Bekah explained. "But she's never come here."

"Then this is kind of an adventure for you." Ester's smile widened. "How do you like it?"

"It's . . . okay." She took another small bite of her sandwich, then opened her thermos.

"I've never been to Paradise before," Ester said. "I'd like to hear all about it."

"There's not much to tell."

Even though Amanda's answers were short and to the point, Ester pressed on. Bekah had to admire her friend's perseverance. Miriam had already started to get bored. "I like your *kapp*," Ester said. "It's different from the ones we wear."

Bekah looked at Amanda's heart-shaped *kapp*, and Amanda put her hand on her *kapp*, but said nothing.

"You could tell them about the differences, and not just the *kapps*," Bekah said. She didn't want Amanda to clam up, not when Ester was getting her to talk a little bit.

She shrugged. "It's not too different." She took another bite of her sandwich.

Bekah swatted at two flies hovering over her lunch box. "I know the buggies are different."

"They are?" Ester asked. "What do they look like?"

"They're gray, and kind of square in the back." Bekah looked to Amanda again. "What else is different, Amanda?"

"There are a lot more Amish people there. But that's about it."

Ester looked at Amanda expectantly, like she was waiting for Amanda to add something else. Miriam was picking her fingernails in between stealing glances at the boys playing baseball. They all waited for Amanda to say something else. When she didn't, they closed the lids of their lunch boxes and got up. Bekah stifled a sigh. Her hopes that Amanda would open up to her friends were dashed.

"We're going to watch the *buwe* play baseball," Ester said. "You want to come with us, Amanda?"

Amanda shook her head. Ester looked at Bekah and shrugged. "Are you coming?"

Bekah glanced at her cousin, and Amanda shook her head. Bekah hid her frustration. She really wanted to join her friends, but she shouldn't desert Amanda. But it wasn't fair that she was stuck sitting here because her cousin didn't want to do anything. "*Nee*," she said, her sigh escaping as she tried to think of a good excuse not to join them. "I've already been hit with the ball. I don't want to get hit again."

"Okay. But if you change your mind, we'll be over there." Miriam pointed across the field where another group of kids was gathered watching the game.

"You can *geh* with your friends," Amanda said, once Ester and Miriam had left. "You don't have to babysit me."

"*Ya*, I do." Bekah hadn't meant to let Amanda know how she felt, but now that she'd already said something, she couldn't stop. The resentment that had been growing toward her cousin for the last couple of days bubbled over. "You've been here two weeks, Amanda. When are you going to stop acting like such a *boppli*?"

As usual, Amanda didn't say anything. Bekah saw her lip quiver, but she didn't care. She got up, ignoring the slight throbbing in her leg. "You're right, I don't have to babysit you. If you want to keep moping around and making everyone else miserable, *geh* right ahead. I'm tired of trying to be your friend. You've made it clear that you don't want to be friends with me." She snatched up her lunch box and stormed off to join Ester and Miriam.

When Bekah reached her friends, she tried not to show how upset she was. She stood next to Ester, giving her friend a tight-lipped smile.

"Where's Amanda?" Ester asked, looking behind her.

"Back there."

"You left her sitting alone?"

Bekah kept her gaze on the game. She didn't have to answer her friend, and she sure wasn't going to worry about her cousin anymore. For all she cared, Amanda could walk back to Paradise. But even though she tried to focus on the game, she felt Ester's eyes on her. "Bekah," she whispered, leaning toward her. "What happened? I've never seen you look so mad."

So much for trying to keep her feelings a secret. "I don't want to talk about it."

"Did Amanda say something to you? She seems really sad. I think she's terribly homesick."

"Would you two be quiet?" Miriam snapped. "Caleb's batting."

Bekah barely heard Miriam's words. She was having enough trouble ignoring the guilt rising within her. Even though she tried not to, she looked over her shoulder at the oak tree. Amanda wasn't there. She gripped the handle of her lunch box. She shouldn't be surprised that Amanda had left. She should go after her. It's what her mother would want her to do. Yet even though she knew checking on Amanda was the right thing to do, Bekah's feet wouldn't move. If Amanda ran away, her mother would blame Bekah. But she'd rather her mother yell at her than get rejected by Amanda again.

"Strike three!" Melvin shouted, lifting up his glove in victory. Caleb threw down his bat, his face pinched with disgust.

Bekah's shoulders slumped. She couldn't even enjoy Caleb striking out.

After Bekah left, Amanda stood up and walked around to the opposite side of the schoolhouse, wanting to be alone.

The small building was bordered by thick woods. She could hear the laughter and squeals of her classmates playing, but the schoolhouse shielded her from seeing them. Her classmates. She shook her head and leaned against the building, the back of her prayer *kapp* pressing against the white siding. None of the kids at this school were her real schoolmates. She thought about her friends back in Paradise. They had started school over a week ago. Did they miss her? She hadn't received a letter from anyone since she left. Maybe they didn't care if she were there or not.

She wiped the sweat from her forehead. Even though she was in the shade, it was still hot outside. She turned and looked down the driveway to the road that ran past the schoolhouse. It would be so easy to leave right now. She could do the same thing that boy had done earlier today. Jacob. At least she thought that was his name. He'd just walked away from school and nothing happened. She could do the same thing. She doubted Bekah would do anything about it. Her cousin was pretty mad at her. Amanda wouldn't have to worry about anyone coming after her, at least not until Bekah got home from school. Maybe this time she would actually make it to the bus station. She still had her money tucked in her sock. She never went anywhere without it, just in case. She could buy a ticket and be on her way to Paradise. It was a perfect plan.

But she shook her head. Her plan wasn't perfect, and she knew it. She would never be able to find the bus station, not on her own. Leaving Middlefield was a stupid fantasy, just like believing her father would come get her soon or that her mother would come back. Each night she prayed that God would help convince her mother to come back home. But with each day that she didn't hear anything, her hope dimmed. Did God even hear her prayers? Did he notice her crying at night? More and more she began to doubt that he did.

None of that changed how she felt about being in Middlefield, though. She might be stuck here, but she didn't have to like it, or do things with Katherine and Bekah, or make friends. Even if she thought Ester was very nice. If things were different, the two of them probably would be friends.

However, she did have to go to school, and *Fraulein* Byler would be calling the class in from recess in a few minutes. She started to head for the other side of the building when she saw something out of the corner of her eye. A flash of movement in the trees in front of her.

She walked toward the woods, gripping her lunch box close to her body. "Hello? Anyone there?" After walking a few yards farther, she decided to turn around. Maybe she'd been imagining things, or she'd seen an animal or bird moving around in there.

"Hey!"

Amanda jumped. She whirled around to see Jacob standing in front of her. When she opened her mouth to say something, he reached out and grabbed her arm, his eyes filled with warning. He held her in a tight, but not painful, grip. She clamped her mouth shut, and he let go of her.

"You're the other new kid, aren't you?" He was a few inches taller than she was, and he peered down at her.

She looked at his hands, which were now at his sides, but halfway curled into fists. She nodded.

"Thought so. You look like you belong here as much as I do."

He had no idea how true his words were. "What are you doing here?"

"In the woods? Or here in Middlefield?" As he talked, his tone relaxed a bit.

"Both, I guess."

"Moved here with my family. But I'm not staying for long. First chance I get, I'm going back to Iowa. That's my real home."

"I'm from Pennsylvania." Finally, someone who understood what she was going through, at least the homesickness part. "How are you going to get back to Iowa?"

He rubbed his finger underneath his nose. "I haven't figured that out yet. But look, I need you to do me a favor. Don't let the teacher know I'm still around here. I can't *geh* home until school's out. I, um, don't really have anywhere else to *geh* until then."

"I won't say anything."

"*Gut*. It won't really matter in a little while anyway, but I still don't want her to know I'm here." He took a deep breath. "My *daed*'s going to be really steamed when he finds out I walked out of school, but I don't care. He can yell at me all he wants. Maybe if he gets mad enough, he'll send me back to Iowa to live with my cousin. Anything is better than here."

"Do you think he'll really do that?"

Jacob didn't say anything for a moment; then he shook his head. "I doubt it. But it's worth a try. Plus, I hate school. I'd rather get in trouble any day than have to sit there and listen to a boring teacher."

Amanda thought he was being harsh. "I think *Fraulein* Byler is nice."

With a scowl Jacob said, "You would. You're a *maedel*. *Maed* always like school."

"I never said I liked school. I just said she was nice."

He shrugged. "Whatever." At the sound of *Fraulein* Byler calling the students to come inside, he took a few steps back into the woods. "Remember what you promised."

She nodded. "I remember." When he disappeared, she turned around and headed for the school. As she saw the teacher, she never thought for a minute about telling on Jacob. Amanda knew how to keep a promise.

After school let out, Amanda ran out of the schoolhouse and didn't bother to wait for Bekah. Her cousin was mad at her, she had made that clear at lunch. So she was surprised to hear her call her name just as she stepped on the side of the road.

"Amanda! Wait up!"

Amanda slowed her steps and waited for Bekah to catch

up. She looked at her cousin. Bekah's cheeks were red from running. They walked for a few minutes without saying anything. Then Bekah finally spoke.

"I'm sorry I called you a *boppli*." She had her head down as she walked. "I shouldn't have done that."

"Don't worry, I'm not going to tell your *mamm*."

Bekah looked at her, one eyebrow lifted. "That's not why I'm apologizing."

"I know." Amanda let out a sigh. "I just don't want you to think I'm going to tattle again."

"Oh. Well, *danki*."

Amanda nodded. "You're welcome."

The girls continued to walk home. After a few moments Bekah suddenly said, "Amanda, if you're so homesick, why don't you call your *daed* and tell him? I'm sure he'd come get you if he knew you were so unhappy here."

Amanda pressed her lips together, not sure what to say. Calling her father wasn't possible. And she couldn't tell Bekah what was going on with her mother. *Daed* wouldn't want that. And even though he told their secret to *Aenti* Margaret and *Onkel* Thomas, she was keeping it. He'd asked her not to tell anyone here about *Mamm*, and she would keep that promise.

"I . . . I can't." She glanced at Bekah, knowing her cousin didn't like her answer. But it was the only answer she could give.

So she was grateful when Bekah didn't pry anymore. She was also surprised. It wasn't like Bekah not to ask a lot of questions. She remembered the first time Bekah came to

Paradise with her family for a visit. Amanda and her parents could barely answer all the questions Bekah had. After giving her a vague answer, Amanda thought Bekah would keep badgering her. Instead, she remained silent as they made their way back home.

When they reached the house, Amanda saw the black-and-white dog again. He was sitting on his haunches at the end of the driveway, like he was waiting for them to come home.

"Roscoe!" Bekah rushed that last few steps to the driveway. She knelt down beside the dog. "Where have you been, *bu*?"

Amanda remembered the dog from the other day when he had come to her in the barn. "Is he your dog?"

Bekah nodded, then shook her head. "He is, and he isn't. He's a stray that's been coming around to all of our *hauss* over the past few years. So he kind of belongs to all of us. I think he's visited every kid at school at least twice, if not more." She rubbed the back of his head. "He's had a bunch of different names, but a couple of years ago Mary Beth Mullet started calling him Roscoe, and the name stuck. It's the one he answers to now."

Amanda set her lunch box on the ground and crouched on the other side of Roscoe. She ran her hand over his soft fur. "Looks like someone gave him a bath." Roscoe barked, and she couldn't help but laugh.

Bekah smiled at her. "I haven't seen him around here in weeks. I wonder what he's been up to?"

"He was here the other day."

"He was? When?"

Amanda told her about Roscoe coming into the barn right before she tried to run away. "I didn't think he was your dog, but he acted like he was right at home."

"That's because he is." Bekah patted him on the nose and stood up. "We should get to the *haus. Mami* will wonder where we are if we're late."

When they reached the house, Amanda turned to Bekah. "Would it be all right if I went to the barn again?"

Bekah shrugged. "I don't see why not. I'll *geh* tell *Mami* we're home."

Amanda walked over to the barn, Roscoe close at her heels. She walked inside, smelling the wonderful scent of fresh hay. After she gave Sparky a little attention, she went and sat on one of the hay bales in the corner. Roscoe joined her, leaning his body against her legs. She stroked his fur, and a sense of peace came over her. For the first time since she arrived in Middlefield, the knot in her stomach that never seemed to go away got a little bit smaller.

While Amanda went to the barn, Bekah went to see her mother. She found her on the front porch, snapping the last of the green beans from their garden. Bekah sat in the chair next to her and snatched a green bean from the metal bowl. "Amanda's home, she went to the barn first."

"I know she enjoys being around the animals. I'm glad

she's taking an interest in something she likes." *Mami* smiled. "So how was your first day back at school?"

Bekah felt a twinge in her leg where Caleb's ball had hit her. She decided not to mention that event to her mother. "Interesting. Amanda's not the only new student at school."

"Oh? There's someone else?"

"*Ya*. A *bu* named Jacob." Bekah also left out the part about him walking out of school. There was no rule that she had to tell her mother everything that happened at school.

"That's nice." Her *mami* picked up a handful of green beans and put them on her lap next to the bowl. She took a bean and snapped each end off, letting the ends fall on the porch. She looked down at the bowl in her lap. "Why don't you finish these up?" She handed the bowl to Bekah.

"All right." Bekah took a bean and started snapping the ends, tossing them onto the front porch as her mother had done. She'd sweep them up later. But when she snapped the green bean in half, she popped one half in her mouth and another in the bowl. There was nothing better than a raw green bean fresh from the garden.

"Don't eat too many of those," her mother warned. "We're having supper in a couple of hours. Plus, I want to have enough to can."

"I won't." Bekah ate another green bean, grinning. At her mother's frown she laughed. "It's my last one, promise."

Her mother brushed off her dark green skirt. "How did Amanda do today?"

"I think she did all right." She thought about how frustrated she'd been with her at lunch. But that had changed on the way home. And when she saw Roscoe, she seemed almost like the Amanda she remembered. "She ate lunch with me and Ester and Miriam."

"That's wonderful. I'd hoped meeting new *maed* would help her."

"*Mami*, why is Amanda really living with us?" The question darted out of Bekah's mouth before she realized it.

Her mother opened her eyes and looked startled at her question. "Bekah, I already told you."

"*Nee*, you didn't. You just said she was staying with us. But you never said why. And you and *Daed* seem really worried about her."

"You don't miss much, do you?"

Bekah smiled a little, not sure if her mother were upset or not. "Nope."

Her mother sighed, leaning back in the chair. "It's true. I'm worried about her, Bekah. But I think I have a right to be. And I'm not surprised she's struggling. She misses her family, and I'm sure she's homesick. But I'm confident she'll come around in time and be her old self. Until she does, she'll need your help."

"I've been trying to help her, *Mami*," Bekah said. "I've asked her to play games with me. I've introduced her to my friends. I tried talking to her. I remembered she likes to read just like I do, so I asked her about her favorite books. She said she didn't have any. She's not interested in spending time with me, so I'm not sure what else I can do."

"It's wonderful that you're working so hard to be a *gut* cousin, and a *gut* friend. I know it's hard, but don't give up on her. She needs you more than she realizes."

Bekah gave her mother a nod, but she wasn't sure her mother was right. If Amanda needed her, Bekah had no idea why. Her cousin seemed determined to keep to herself.

Her mother got up from the chair. "When you're finished with the beans, bring them into the kitchen."

Bekah nodded. "Sure. Are you going to start supper?"

"In a little while. Right now I'm going to check on the cake I put in the oven."

"Cake?" Bekah's mouth started to water. "What kind?"

Her mother smiled. "Guess."

"Chocolate?"

"With white frosting." Her mother winked and went inside.

"Yum," Bekah said. Her favorite flavor of cake with her favorite frosting! Even though Caleb had hit her with a baseball and she had gotten into a little fight with Amanda, it was turning out to be a pretty okay day. Bekah finished snapping the beans, sneaking a few more despite promising her mother she wouldn't. She couldn't help it; they were too tempting. When she finished she got the broom and swept up the ends, leaving the porch tidy. She went inside to the kitchen. Her mother wasn't there, but the room was filled with the delicious aroma of the cake, which was sitting in a metal pan on the counter. She put the bowl on the kitchen table and walked over to the cake, leaning forward and breathing in the chocolaty smell.

She went to the sink and washed her hands, peeking out the kitchen window, which faced the front yard. She had just rinsed the last traces of soap off her hands when she spied a large orange-and-white moving truck backing into the driveway next door.

Eleven

A MOVING truck! Bekah left the kitchen and went to the back porch. She had a better view of the house from here. The truck had backed all the way up to the house. Now Bekah could see the minivan had been parked on the street. A driver got out of the cab at the same time the old man came outside. Bekah watched as another man exited the passenger side and joined the other two. They opened the back of the truck and pulled out a silver ramp. The two men then brought a brown couch out of the truck and carried it into the house. She could hear the old man barking orders to them as they worked.

Amanda joined Bekah on the porch. "Looks like he's moving in."

"Ya." Finally.

"I think Roscoe's hungry." Amanda put her hand on the dog's head.

Bekah looked down at Roscoe, who was sitting on the

porch, looking up at her. He cocked his head to the side. "I think you're right. You can go inside and get a couple of those old whipped topping bowls *Mami*'s always saving. They're in the cupboard by the sink. I usually use those for his food and water bowls when he comes around."

"Do you have any dog food?"

"*Nee*, but I'm sure we can give him some scraps from supper."

"All right." Amanda gave Roscoe one more pat before going inside.

Bekah turned her attention back to the moving truck. Roscoe stayed on the back porch, waiting for Amanda to return. She came back in a few minutes with a white plastic bowl filled with water. Roscoe lapped at it while the men finished moving. The old man didn't have much furniture—a dresser, a table and four chairs, the couch, and a bed. She supposed that was all someone needed anyway.

As soon as the moving truck pulled out, *Mami* called them in for supper. But later after the meal, when Amanda and Bekah brought out the leftovers that *Mami* said they could give to Roscoe, he was nowhere in sight.

"Where did he *geh*?" Amanda asked, looking upset.

Bekah shrugged. "He does this all the time. Shows up for a little while, then leaves. He'll be back."

"When?"

"I don't know. Roscoe keeps his own schedule."

Amanda's shoulder's drooped "Oh. I was hoping he would stick around."

Bekah could see the sadness return to her cousin's eyes. "He will, Amanda. Don't worry. Like I said, he does this all the time. I bet he'll be back tomorrow."

But Amanda didn't seem convinced. "I'm going inside." She turned and left.

Bekah sighed. She hoped for Amanda's sake that Roscoe would come back soon. Being around the dog seemed to help her feel better.

However, Roscoe didn't return over the next couple of days, and Amanda continued to be quiet, although not as sullen as before. She had started eating more, but she wasn't talking very much to anyone. On Wednesday after work, Katherine had even brought home some yarn and a crochet hook she'd purchased from a discount store. But when she offered to show Amanda how to crochet, Amanda refused to talk or do anything.

By Thursday, *Fraulein* Byler had started giving homework, and Bekah had a reading assignment to finish. She decided to do her reading under the oak tree near the pond. Soon enough the weather would turn cold, and there wouldn't be many days left when she could do her homework outside. Amanda chose to stay inside, as usual. Bekah didn't bother to try to change her mind.

She walked to the tree and sat down underneath the shade, digging her bare toes into the cool grass. She tried not to remember the last time she'd sat underneath this tree, attempting to read. She glanced around, making sure Caleb wasn't lurking somewhere, even though he hadn't shown up at her house since the day they had both snooped next door. A couple of birds chirped in the branches above. Bekah drew her knees to her chest and opened her book. But before she started the reading selection, she looked at the house next door. She had a good view of the neighbor's backyard. Her father still hadn't spoken to the old man, not since that first short conversation they'd had. According to *Daed*, the man was gone before sunrise and didn't return until late. But he must have been home early today, since the minivan was in the driveway.

She had read two paragraphs when Roscoe suddenly appeared. Bekah set down the book and started petting the dog. "I know someone who's going to be happy to see you." She stood up. "Now, stay while I *geh* get Amanda." But as soon as she started for the house, Roscoe began sniffing around the yard. He went to the old swing set, his muzzle close to the ground.

"Roscoe, I told you to stay!" Bekah came back and tried to get him to sit, but he went to the pond instead and lapped at the water. Great. He wasn't listening to her. She hoped he at least stayed in the yard. She'd hate to go get Amanda and bring her outside, only to see that Roscoe had taken off again. Bekah hurried toward the house, looking over her shoulder halfway. She saw the dog trotting over to the yard next door.

"Roscoe, *nee*!" She turned around and hurried to the yard, crossing over the boundary just in time to see the dog pawing at the ground. She started to run. "Stop it!" But Roscoe ignored her.

Then she saw the hole. She paused. It was pretty deep, and he couldn't have dug it that quickly. The hole must have been there before. Bekah glanced over the yard, noticing how short the grass was. A few feet away she saw another hole. Then a third. She realized that there were several holes within a few yards of each other. Had Roscoe dug all these? She remembered the night she'd seen the old man out here digging. Maybe they were his holes. How many holes had he dug? Just from the quick glance she could see at least six. The more she thought about it, the more convinced she was that the holes weren't Roscoe's. He had never dug up her yard, or anyone else's that she knew. What was that guy burying out here?

The sound of a screen door slamming shut caused her head to snap up. The old man came barreling outside, straight toward Roscoe. "Get away from there!" He lifted his leg as if to kick the dog.

"*Nee*!" Bekah jumped in front of him, and the man froze. "Don't hurt him!"

"Then get your dog off my property!"

She didn't bother to tell him Roscoe wasn't exactly her dog. She didn't want to make him even angrier. She bent down and pushed Roscoe on the rump. "*Halt*, Roscoe. Please, stop."

As if he understood, Roscoe suddenly stopped digging and sat down next to her. He looked up, his tongue lolling out of his mouth, his tail wagging against the grass.

"Get out of my yard. Both of you." The old man looked

at her, his eyes filled with anger. He had more wrinkles than she had ever seen, a hunched back, and sallow skin. Seeing him up close made a shiver go down her spine. He didn't seem like a kindly old man right now.

"I'm sorry." Her voice trembled, but she couldn't help it. He was scary.

He continued to glare at her. "I don't wanna hear it. I want you out of my yard. And if you and your mutt ever cross my property line again, I'm calling the police! Now get!" The old man raised his arm and pointed to Bekah's house.

Bekah nodded and ran away. Fortunately, Roscoe followed close behind. She fled to the tree, snatched her book, and ran inside the house. Roscoe stopped and waited on the porch. He knew he wasn't allowed to come in. Bekah's chest heaved. She looked at Roscoe through the screen door. "Don't go to that mean old man's *haus* again."

Roscoe barked; then he left. She watched to see if he went next door again, but the dog went through the front yard and trotted down the road, no doubt visiting another family, unaffected by their encounter with her new neighbor.

Bekah blew out a deep breath. Good thing she hadn't told Amanda that Roscoe was here. She didn't need her cousin to be afraid of the old man. That would give her another reason to not like living here. Catching her breath, she went into the living room, trying to pretend everything was normal. She plopped down on the couch and opened her book, but her hands were shaking. She tried forcing herself to focus on her homework, but she couldn't concentrate. Finally she gave up and snapped the book shut. All she could think about was how the old man had threatened to call the police. Well, he wouldn't have to worry about doing that. She didn't want to have anything to do with him anymore.

By the time supper rolled around, Bekah had calmed down. As long as she kept her distance from the old man, she wouldn't have anything to worry about. *Daed* wasn't home by suppertime, and *Mami* explained that he would be coming home late because he was helping one of their neighbors repair his barn. Bekah didn't tell her mother about the old man's threat. She didn't want her to worry or, worse, get upset because Bekah had gone next door after being told not to.

Later that night *Mami* helped Amanda with a math homework assignment she was having trouble with. A storm was blowing in, and it was already dark by the time Bekah went upstairs. Even though it was still warm in her bedroom, the evening was cooler than it had been in a long while, and someone had closed the window. She walked over and opened it again, just as a flash of lightning lit up the sky. In that moment, she caught a glimpse of her neighbor's backyard. The old man was out there, and he was digging again. Remembering the way he'd yelled at her, she shut the curtains tight. But that didn't keep her from wondering what he was burying beneath the dirt in his backyard. She was curious, but she was also too scared to find out.

They were walking home after school. Miriam had joned them. She was visiting her aunt today, who lived on the way to Bekah's house. Bekah nodded at something Miriam said, as she looked around. Amanda was several feet behind her. Usually they walked together, but for some reason she didn't join Bekah and Miriam. That was okay. Bekah had been dying to tell someone about what had happened yesterday, and she decided to confide in Miriam. Her friend had never told any of Bekah's secrets, not that she had many, and never one like this. "But you can't tell anyone. Not a single soul. Promise?"

Miriam nodded. "I promise. But why don't you want me to say anything? This is some exciting stuff."

"Because he's mean, and I don't know for sure what he's doing back there. If he finds out I'm telling people what he does at night, he might come after me. He's already threatened to call the police."

Miriam sucked in a breath. "The police?"

Bekah nodded. "But he won't, because I'm leaving him alone."

"But don't you want to find out what he's burying? I know I would if he were my neighbor."

Dread gathered inside Bekah. Now Miriam seemed too excited and too curious about this whole thing. Maybe she should have kept her mouth shut. But it was too late now. "Miriam, please. Just forget about it. I don't want anyone else to find out. My parents don't even know."

"Okay, I'll keep quiet."

They continued down the road a few more yards, not saying anything. Then Miriam turned to her. "I can't stand it anymore. You have to tell me. How many holes does he have in his yard?"

"Six, maybe seven. I'm not sure, I didn't get a good look. He might dig some during the day. I didn't stop to count them, though. I just got out of his yard, like he said."

"Thank goodness Roscoe listened too. It would be awful if something happened to him."

"I know." Bekah clutched her schoolbooks to her chest. "I knew something was mysterious over there, but I didn't think he was downright mean." He was nearly as scary as the tattooed man. At least that man had never come back. "If it's all right with you, I don't want to talk about this anymore."

Miriam nodded, her expression grave. "I understand."

Bekah snuck a glance over her shoulder and noticed Amanda had fallen even farther behind. She looked at her friend. "I don't know why Amanda isn't walking with us."

Miriam rolled her eyes. "I do—there's something wrong with her! I tried talking to her earlier, and she didn't say anything back. I think she's being rude. I don't see how you can stand her."

Bekah frowned at her friend. "Don't be so hard on her, Miriam." Miriam didn't know what her cousin was struggling with. If she did, she'd be a lot nicer. "She's homesick. You would be too, if you were away from your parents for a couple of weeks."

"I guess." Miriam looked behind her. "But she's always so mopey. Can't she see that she brings everyone down? Who wants to be around someone who's so sad all the time?"

Bekah looked at her friend, incredulous. Even though they had known each other since they were little kids, she hadn't realized how insensitive Miriam could be. She suddenly didn't want to walk with her anymore, and she wished she hadn't told her about the old man. Quickening her steps she said, "I've got to get home. I'll see you at church on Sunday." She looked over her shoulder and whispered. "Remember, don't tell anyone."

"I already said I wouldn't." A look of irritation crossed Miriam's features. "You don't have to keep telling me. I'm not *dumm,* you know. And I have to get to my *aenti*'s anyway." Miriam broke into a jog and left Bekah behind.

Relieved that Miriam had left, Bekah slowed down, then turned and went to Amanda. A few moments later she fell into step beside her cousin.

"Why aren't you walking with your friend anymore?" Amanda asked.

Because she's mean. I just hope she doesn't have a big mouth too. "She had to leave. Her *aenti* is expecting her. Besides, I wanted to walk with you."

"Oh." Amanda looked surprised. "Well, *danki* for walking with me."

As they continued walking home, Bekah regarded Amanda. Maybe she should tell Amanda about what happened yesterday. At least give her some warning about staying away from the old man. But then again, she already regretted telling Miriam, and she didn't want to upset Amanda, especially since she was starting to act like she was a little more comfortable staying here. Bekah didn't want to ruin that.

"What do you think about Jacob?" Amanda suddenly asked.

Bekah thought about the new boy who had walked out of school on the first day. He had come back the next day, and he'd been causing problems for *Fraulein* Byler ever since. "I don't know why he can't behave," she said. "Everyone else does. Well, most everyone." Caleb had to stay after school today for not turning in a homework assignment. But that was nothing compared to Jacob walking out of school or falling asleep in class, snoring loud enough for everyone to hear. "Why do you ask?"

"I think he's a lot like me," Amanda said.

Bekah scoffed. "He's nothing like you, Amanda. You do your schoolwork. You don't cause any trouble."

Amanda looked down. "I cause lots of people trouble."

Bekah thought about *Aenti* Caroline. Had Amanda's mother left because of something Amanda had done? Bekah couldn't imagine that was true. She shook her head. "*Nee*, you don't."

"I think Jacob misses his friends. It's hard to live in a new place."

"I'm sure it is."

Her cousin quickened her steps. They were almost home. "I'll be inside in a little while," she said, heading for the barn like she did every day after school now. Roscoe had even come by a couple of times, following her inside. He seemed to be hanging around a lot more since Amanda had arrived.

When Bekah walked through the front door, she could smell the scent of fresh bread. Her stomach growled. She was ready for a snack—she was always starving by the time she got home. She walked into the kitchen where her mother was pulling two loaves out of the oven. She put her books and lunch box on the table. "That smells *gut, Mami.*"

Her mother glanced over her shoulder. "Are you hungry? I can fix you a slice."

"*Ya*. I'd like some."

As her mother cut Bekah a slice of piping hot bread, she asked, "Do you think Amanda would like a piece too?"

Bekah shrugged. "I don't know. She's in the barn again. Want me to run out there and ask?"

Her mother hesitated, then shook her head. "*Nee*. She'll come inside when she's ready." She brought Bekah a piece of the bread, the steam still rising from the slice. "Butter?"

"*Nee*. I'd like it plain today."

Her mother chuckled. "I never know with you."

She picked up the bread, realized it was too hot to eat, then set it down on the plate.

Her mother sat next to her. "Has Amanda made any friends at school?"

"Not really. She still eats lunch with me and a couple of my friends, but she doesn't say much."

"Oh." Her mother sighed. "Well, making friends does take time. Maybe in a few weeks she'll feel more comfortable."

But Bekah wondered if Amanda would ever be happy. How could she be, with her mother gone? "*Mami*, why did *Aenti* leave *Onkel*?"

Her mother's mouth dropped open. "How did you know about that?"

Her cheeks heated. She hadn't meant to voice the question out loud. But now that it was out in the open, she wanted answers. She'd been wondering about this long enough. "I heard you and *Daed* talking."

"You were eavesdropping? What did I tell you about spying, Bekah?"

"I'm sorry. I know I'm not supposed to listen to your conversations. But it was right after Amanda ran away, and I knew something was really wrong. I wanted to know what happened, and when I heard you and *Daed* talking about it in the living room . . ."

Her mother sighed, her shoulders slumping. "Your *vatter* won't be happy with me for telling you. But I can't lie to you, Bekah. And I suppose I should have told you the real story before she came here. Maybe that would have made a difference. But I was hoping you wouldn't have to find out. And we didn't want you treating Amanda any differently than before. Which you haven't, except when I've asked you to." *Mami* touched the top of Bekah's hand. "Remember that what I'm about to tell you is a secret. You can't tell anyone. And whatever you do, don't let Amanda find out that you know about this. She hasn't said much of anything about *Aenti* Caroline, so I don't think she wants to discuss it."

"I promise." Bekah sat up straighter in the chair, understanding the seriousness of what her mother was about to tell her. She wanted her mother to know she could trust her.

Her mother let out a long breath. "*Aenti* Caroline left Amanda and your *Onkel* Ezra about three months ago. Ezra said she had been acting strange and distant even before that. One day Amanda came home from a friend's house, and her mother wasn't there. She found a note telling her and *Onkel* Ezra that she couldn't stay in Paradise anymore and that she didn't want to be Amish." Her mother's face fell. "She moved in with some Yankee friends about an hour from Paradise. Your *onkel* has tried to talk her into coming back home, but she said she doesn't want to. She told him that she should have never gotten married or joined the church."

Bekah's heart filled with sadness. "How could she say something like that?"

Her mother shrugged. "I'm not sure, but it's possible she's depressed."

"Depressed? About what?"

"About a year ago *Aenti* Caroline was going to have a *boppli*. But then, the *boppli* died, before it was born. She was very, very sad when that happened."

"That's awful. Does Amanda know?"

"*Nee*. We didn't even know until Ezra told us after Caroline left. He said she hadn't been the same since then. About a month ago he wrote us a letter asking if we could keep Amanda here with us until he can convince your *aenti* to come back home. He thinks she's still upset over losing the *boppli*."

"But I don't understand. If she's upset over the *boppli*, why would she leave? Wouldn't she want to be with *Onkel* Ezra and Amanda? Wouldn't they make her feel better?"

Her mother rubbed her finger against the top of the kitchen table. "Sometimes when people are depressed, they don't think straight. They'll sometimes do strange things, like your *aenti* leaving her family. It's hard to explain."

"I think I understand." Bekah thought about Amanda, and how strange she'd been acting since arriving in Middlefield. Was her cousin depressed too? Bekah thought she might be.

"When your *Onkel* Ezra contacted us, your *daed* and I discussed it, and we agreed that it would be better for Amanda to be away from everything going on back home. With her here, Ezra can focus on helping *Aenti* Caroline. We thought that since Amanda doesn't have any brothers or sisters, she could spend time with you and your friends, and that might help keep her mind off of her mother being gone. But that doesn't seem to be working out very well."

Bekah was still trying to wrap her mind around the fact that her *aenti* had left her *onkel* and moved in with people who weren't Amish. She had never heard of that happening before. When the Amish married, they married for life. There was no separation or divorce. At least that's what she'd been taught all her life. And even if she were depressed, how could her *aenti* leave Amanda? Her own daughter? Bekah didn't want to imagine what her life would be like without *Mami* in it.

"So you see why I wanted you to help her as much as you could," *Mami* said. "And I'm very grateful for what you've done for her. But I realize now that we can't make everything right for Amanda, even though we want to. I think this is something we're going to have to pray long and hard about, and put into God's hands. He can help both Amanda and her mother heal."

Bekah tapped her finger against her chin, thinking. She tried to imagine what she would do if she were in Amanda's place. "Has Amanda written to *Aenti* Caroline or *Onkel* Ezra? Maybe if she wrote a letter to them it might make her feel better. Or at least a little closer to her *mami* and *daed*."

"I'm not sure if she's done that or not. But I think that's a *gut* idea. Maybe writing them a letter might help her with the homesickness."

"I could sit down and write with her," Bekah volunteered. "I haven't written to *Grossmami* in a while." Bekah's grandparents lived in Holmes County, where her mother was from. She was long overdue to send her grandmother a letter.

"I think both Amanda and your *grossmami* would like that." Her mother reached out and touched Bekah's hand. "I'm glad we talked about this, Bekah. You're growing up to be quite a young *fraa*." She rose from the table and sliced another piece of bread.

Bekah smiled, happy that her *mami* had confided in her and that she had earned her trust. "I'll make sure to say a special prayer for *Aenti* Caroline tonight."

Her mother nodded and smiled back. "I will too, Bekah."

Twelve

Once her mother had gone upstairs, Bekah took her bread and went outside. She sat down and ate the delicious slice on the front porch, enjoying what was left of the afternoon. A buggy went by her house and she waved, even though she didn't recognize the driver. It never hurt to be friendly. Then she glanced next door and saw the minivan in the driveway. Except where her new neighbor was concerned. The old man was home. That made her think about the holes in the backyard, something she immediately put out of her mind. *I don't care what he's doing back there. It's none of my business.*

She continued to eat, waiting for Amanda to come in from the barn. Even though she had Sparky out there and sometimes Roscoe, she was still spending too much time alone. Bekah didn't think that was a good idea, especially now that she knew about *Aenti* Caroline. The more she thought about it, the more convinced she was that Amanda were also depressed. Bekah didn't want her cousin to do something crazy again, like when she tried to run away.

Bekah took another bite of the bread, her mind whirring. Maybe she and her mother were thinking about this in the wrong way. Maybe they were all being too nice, letting Amanda have her own way about everything. Perhaps the only way to get Amanda to spend time with other people was to *make* her. An idea occurred to her. Bekah polished off her bread and ran upstairs to her room. She went to her closet and found her old orange Frisbee. She held the slightly warped toy in her hand. She hadn't played with it in years, mostly because she didn't have anyone to play with. Now she did, and as sure as her name was Rebekah Elizabeth Yoder, she was going to throw it around a few times with Amanda. Whether her cousin wanted to or not.

She dashed into the barn, holding the Frisbee behind her back.

When she walked in, she saw Amanda sitting on the hay bale, staring at her feet. She went over to her cousin and plopped down. "Okay, Amanda. You and I are gonna have a little talk."

Amanda looked at her, frowning. "About what?"

"You spend way too much time in this barn. And way too much time alone. But that's gonna change." Bekah grinned and held out the Frisbee.

Her cousin looked at it, her frown deepening.

"What, you haven't seen a Frisbee before?"

"Of course I have. I even have one at home."

"Great! Then I won't have to show you how to play."

Amanda shook her head. "I don't want to play. I was just going inside to do my homework. I have lots to finish."

Bekah shook her head. "Nope. That excuse won't work. You'll have plenty of time to do homework tonight. You can't stay locked up in my bedroom or out in this smelly barn all the time."

"There's nothing wrong with the way the barn smells."

"That's a matter of opinion." Bekah wrinkled her nose. "Amanda, there's so much fun stuff we can do together—Frisbee, for starters. Plus, you know Katherine wants to teach you how to crochet, and *Mami* said she'd show you how to make that delicious white pie we had the other day that you said you liked."

Amanda looked away. "That's okay." Her voice was low. "She doesn't have to do that. Neither does Katherine."

"But they *want* to." Bekah stood in front of her cousin. "We all want to do things with you, Amanda. But we can't when you don't let us." She twisted the stiff plastic edge of the Frisbee between her fingers. "And when we're done playing Frisbee, you're going to write a letter to your *mami* and *daed*."

Amanda's eyes widened. "*Nee*, I'm not going to do that."

"Not by yourself, you aren't. I owe my *grossmami* a letter. So we can do that together too."

Amanda looked away again, not saying anything. When Bekah grew tired of waiting, she tapped her on the head with the Frisbee.

Amanda looked up at her. "Stop that!"

Bekah tapped her again. "*Nee*. Not until you play with me."

"I—"

Tap.

"—don't—"

Tap.

"—want—"

Tap.

"—to—"

Tap. Tap.

"All right, fine!" Amanda scowled and jumped up from the hay bale. "I'll *geh* outside with you. Then will you leave me alone?"

Smiling, Bekah nodded. "I will. But only after you write the letter."

Amanda shook her head. She'd only said she'd go outside so Bekah would quit bugging her. She never promised she'd actually *play* with Bekah. Her cousin must have realized that because she clenched her fist and marched over to her, stomping past and picking up the Frisbee. Then she stomped back and stood in front of Amanda.

"Why won't you catch it?"

"I told you I don't want to play." And it was the truth. She didn't. She wanted to be alone. Either in the barn or upstairs in Bekah's bedroom—she didn't care. After a while, she always fell asleep, making the time go faster until the day her father came to get her, whenever that would be. The last thing she wanted to do was play with Bekah. Or become friends with her friends. Or sit down with her aunt and uncle and enjoy herself. How could she, when her father was alone back in Paradise? When seeing Bekah and her mother talking and laughing made her heart twist inside? She wished she were anywhere but here! But she had no escape. She had tried that, and they had dragged her right back here.

Then she thought about how much she liked it when Roscoe came around. And how nice Ester was to her at school. And the way *Aenti* Margaret always hugged her before she went to bed. She shook her head, trying to erase them from her mind. She didn't want to think about the good things in Middlefield.

Bekah let out a huffy breath. She thrust the Frisbee at Amanda. "Just throw it once. That's all I'm asking."

"*Nee.*"

"One time. Then I'll leave you alone for the rest of the day."

That sounded appealing. Amanda dropped her arms. "Just one time?"

Bekah nodded.

"And I won't have to write the letter?"

"*Nee*. Not today."

"Not ever."

Her cousin shook her head. "I'm not promising that." She held out the Frisbee again. "*Geh* on. One time, then I have to get inside and help *Mami* with supper. You can *geh* lock yourself up in the room or the barn or anywhere else you want."

Amanda heard the irritation in Bekah's voice, and a tiny pang of guilt formed in her. But she shoved it away. She didn't ask to come here, didn't ask for Bekah to have to be nice to her, or her aunt to tell her she understood. Her aunt didn't really understand anything. *She* didn't have a mother who abandoned her, and a father who sent her away because she was too much trouble. Her anger churning, she snatched the Frisbee out of Bekah's hand and flung it as hard as she could. It sailed in the air, landing in the next-door neighbor's yard. "There. I did it. Happy now?"

Bekah eyes suddenly grew wide. "What did you do that for? Now I have to *geh* get it."

"So?"

Bekah looked over her shoulder, licking her bottom lip. "Um, *Daed* said not to *geh* next door, remember?"

Amanda shrugged, although she had forgotten about her uncle's warning. "Just leave it in his yard."

"I can't do that." Bekah twisted her fingers together. "It's my Frisbee. He'll be mad if I leave it there."

"Who?"

"The old man." Bekah looked at her like she was an idiot.

"Fine." Amanda clenched her fists. She and Bekah could argue about this for the rest of the afternoon. "I'll *geh* get it."

Bekah's brows raised in surprise as Amanda strode past her. "Wait. I'll come with you."

Amanda didn't care if Bekah came or not. She dashed into the backyard and snatched the Frisbee. She turned around, expecting Bekah to be right behind her. Instead, she was by the edge of the house, as if she were searching for something. When Amanda went to her, her bare foot landed on something soft. She looked down. In the green grass she saw a patch of dirt, as if someone had covered a hole. Stepping around it, she walked over to Bekah.

"What are you doing?" she said, automatically lowering her voice.

"Checking something real quick." Bekah glanced around, then squatted down on the ground. She was near the edge of the house, in the corner by what would be a flower bed. Instead, there were a bunch of weeds. Amanda wondered why her cousin would be interested in those.

"I thought you said we weren't supposed to be over here."

"We're not." Bekah looked at her, a mix of excitement and panic in her eyes. "This will only take a minute. I promise. Then we'll leave." She looked down again. "This is the only chance I have to check it out."

"Check what out?" Confused, Amanda tapped Bekah on the shoulder. "What are you talking about?"

"Does it look like someone dug something here?" Bekah glanced up at Amanda.

Amanda rolled her shoulders, then looked down. She didn't like the idea of disobeying her uncle's wishes. "I don't know. We should leave, Bekah."

"Just one more minute."

"I'm going back home." But when she moved to leave, Bekah grabbed the skirt of her dress. Amanda had to stay or the hem would rip, and she didn't want to ask her aunt to sew it up. She'd already been given one dress. She didn't want anyone feeling sorry for her anymore. "Hey! What are you doing?"

"Come down here." Bekah tugged again.

Amanda dropped to her knees. "What?" she huffed.

"Look. A couple of weeks ago when Caleb was here, we saw this." Bekah pointed at a patch of dirt, similar to the one Amanda had stepped on. "See how the rest of this patch is weeds? Why would there be only one dirt spot?"

"There isn't." Amanda pointed at a second one several inches away. "See? Here's another one."

"That's what I wanted you to look at." Her tone grew excited. "That wasn't here when Caleb and I were looking around."

"So?"

"There are more holes here. He's been digging in the flower beds too, not just the yard."

"Who?"

"The old man. Aren't you listening to me?"

"*Ya*, but you're not making sense. He's digging holes in his yard?"

She nodded. "I saw a bunch of them yesterday."

Amanda peered over Bekah's shoulder and saw what she was talking about. She fought her curiosity, but she couldn't help it. "I found another spot over there."

"You did?" Bekah's eyes grew wide with excitement. "Where?"

"By the Frisbee." Amanda stood. "I'll show you."

The girls walked to the back of the yard, near the rickety split-rail fence that edged the back of the old man's yard. Amanda pushed back the grass with her toe. "It's right here somewhere . . . there." She pointed to the dirt while Bekah bent down and examined it.

"You're right. It's just like the other two." Bekah shot up and looked at Amanda. "Why would he do that? I can see digging one or two holes, but there must be seven or eight just around here."

Although she was wondering the same thing, Amanda didn't see the big deal. "That's his business, I guess."

"But aren't you the least bit curious? The holes are all small. And if he's going to take the trouble to dig them, then why not cut the grass or clean out the flower bed?"

"I don't—"

"Hey!"

Both girls spun around to see the old man storming toward them, his grizzled face red with rage. Amanda felt Bekah's hand clutch her upper arm.

"What are you two doing in my yard?" The man stopped right in front of them. He glared at them with jaundiced eyes.

Amanda couldn't speak. He was mean and angry looking. Now she wished she'd never thrown the Frisbee over here.

Bekah let go of Amanda. "We were just getting our Frisbee," she said.

"Keep your toys in your own yard. I don't want you coming over here." He put his hands on his hips and scowled. Then he narrowed his eyes. "You were over here the other day with your dog. Didn't I tell you I'd call the police if I saw you here again?"

"B-but we're your neighbors." Bekah pointed to her house. Amanda noticed her hand shook. "I'm Rebekah Yoder, and this is—"

"I don't care who you are. Now, get!" The man flung out his arms and walked toward them. "And if you come back again, I really will call the cops!"

Amanda and Bekah turned and ran toward the house. Amanda dropped the Frisbee on the back porch and dashed into the kitchen, Bekah close behind. Her *Aenti* Margaret was in the kitchen mixing something in a bowl. She stopped when both girls plopped down at the kitchen table, their chests heaving from running.

Aenti Margaret came over to them, the bowl in the crook of her arm. "Is something wrong?"

Amanda looked at Bekah. Her cousin's face was flushed, and a remnant of fear shone in her eyes. She didn't say anything, waiting to see what Bekah would tell her mother. After a long moment, Bekah turned and looked up at *Aenti* Margaret.

"Amanda and I were playing Frisbee, and it flew into the neighbor's yard. We went to *geh* get it, and he yelled at us." Bekah paused. "He said he would call the police if we were ever over there again."

Her mother's mouth set in a thin, grim line. "He did, did he?"

"*Ya.*"

When her aunt looked at her, Amanda nodded in agreement. "He was really angry, *Aenti.*"

Her mother picked up the wooden spoon and started stirring with lightning fast strokes. "It is his property," she said, through tight lips. "So you better do as he says, *maed.* Your father already warned you not to *geh* over there."

"But we had to get the Frisbee," Bekah said.

"Then make sure the Frisbee—and any other toy—doesn't wind up in his yard. And if for some reason you have to *geh* over there, come get your father or me. We'll take care of it. I don't want you bothering him anymore."

Bekah and Amanda both nodded. "We won't."

"*Gut.* Now *geh* wash your hands and help me with supper. I'm making chicken and dumplings, with apple pie for dessert. You two can cut up the apples for me."

Amanda and Bekah both went into the bathroom and shut the door. Bekah washed her hands first. Amanda noticed that her cousin had stopped shaking.

"What did he mean about you being over there before? And with what dog? Was Roscoe with you?"

Bekah rinsed her hands and reached for the towel on the rack near the sink. "Roscoe ran over there yesterday. The old man was being mean to him, so I went to get him."

"And he said he'd call the police?"

Bekah nodded, her lips pressed together.

Amanda shook her head. "Then why would you *geh* over there again?"

"To get the Frisbee, remember?"

"*Ya*, but all you had to do was get the Frisbee and come back." Amanda lowered her voice. "You shouldn't have stayed over there, snooping around his yard."

"I know." Bekah sighed. "I can't help it, Amanda. I've been dying to find out what he's burying over there. I tried not to think about it, but when I was in his yard . . . I just wanted to take a quick look. I didn't think we'd get caught."

"We should mind our own business." Amanda reached for the soap and lathered her hands. "Your *mamm* is right, we need to leave him and his yard alone." She rinsed off the soap and dried her hands on the towel. "Besides, who says he's burying anything?" Amanda hung the towel back on the rack.

"Why else would he be digging up his yard?" Bekah said. "Besides, you saw how mad he was about us being there. He's hiding something. He has to be."

Amanda didn't have an answer to that. A shiver passed through her as she thought about what he might be burying in those small holes. Bones? No, that couldn't be it. That was too creepy. But she kept seeing the old man's face in her mind. He definitely was creepy. "What if he's doing something illegal? Should we tell? Or maybe we should be the ones to call the police on him."

Bekah shook her head. "If we tell *Mami*, she'll just tell us the same thing: to stay away and mind our own business."

"Which we should do."

Bekah's expression grew more serious than Amanda had ever seen it. She nodded. "Whatever you do, don't tell anyone about the holes. Not my parents, not our friends at school, no one."

Amanda thought that would be easy to do, considering she didn't have any friends.

"Promise me." Bekah took a step forward. "This is our secret, okay?"

Amanda realized she had been asked to keep a lot of secrets lately. First her father wanted her not to say anything about her mother; then Jacob hadn't wanted her to tell the teacher he was hiding in the woods. Now Bekah wanted her to keep another secret. She had to admit it felt good to know people felt they could trust her. "Okay. I promise I won't say anything."

Bekah relaxed and opened the bathroom door. "We better get back and start cutting apples before *Mami* gets suspicious."

Amanda followed Bekah, still thinking about the old man and the holes in the yard. Now that she knew about them, she could understand why Bekah had a hard time keeping her curiosity in check. It was hard not to wonder what was going on next door. She had promised Bekah she wouldn't say anything, and she would keep her word. But had she and Bekah made the right decision? She wasn't completely sure.

Amanda sat at the kitchen table and picked up a red apple. With a paring knife she started to peel it, then cut it into slices like her mother had taught her. She had always liked helping *Mamm* in the kitchen; it was one of the things she missed most about her. But while she felt a little sad, the pain wasn't as sharp as it normally was when she thought about her mother. And it was only when she finished peeling her second apple and had handed it to her aunt that she remembered her vow not to do anything with the Yoder family.

Thirteen

For the next two days, after the sun went down and everyone was in bed, Bekah got up and went to her window. Despite her mother's warnings, she couldn't help herself. Now that she had seen the holes, she had to know what was going on. But she couldn't get caught, not by her parents and certainly not by the old man. Keeping vigil here every night since she and Amanda had been caught in his backyard seemed to be the safest way to monitor what he was doing. What better time to bury something than under the cover of darkness? And tonight was perfect, since the full moon was casting its silvery light outside. Still, she felt a little guilty when she took her post.

But by Sunday night her diligence seemed pointless. He hadn't come outside, not even once. That disappointed her, almost as much as seeing Miriam in church that morning. Her friend had ignored Bekah completely after the church service, something she had never done before. Bekah couldn't figure out why Miriam was mad at her. As far as she knew she hadn't done anything wrong.

The summer heat had finally broken and it had turned cooler this evening. She shivered as she crouched down in front of the window, putting Miriam out of her mind. She didn't know if the old man could see her this far away, but she wasn't taking any chances. Maybe tonight would be the night he would make another move. Perhaps he would dig another hole and bury something else. Or he might pull out something he'd already buried. Oh, would she love to see that! She felt like Nancy Drew solving one of her mysteries—although it was hard to solve a mystery from the safety of her window. But sneaking over there was out now. She'd already been caught twice in the old man's yard, like he had been standing guard at the window. She didn't want to think what would happen if she got caught a third time. She would keep her distance and watch from her bedroom.

"What are you doing?"

Bekah turned around to see Amanda sitting up in bed. *Uh oh.* She had thought her cousin was asleep. No reason to lie about her activities, though. Amanda knew the whole story. "I'm watching," she said, keeping her voice low. Her parent's bedroom was just down the hall, and she didn't want them to know she was still up.

Amanda got up and padded over to the window. "I thought you said we were minding our own business?"

"We are, sort of." She glanced at her cousin, who was wearing an old, pale blue nightgown. She'd have to remember to ask *Mami* to make her another nightgown. "I just want to see if he is doing any digging tonight."

"How is that minding our own business?"

Bekah looked at her. She didn't have an answer for that.

Amanda stood on her tiptoes and peered over Bekah's shoulder. "Is he outside?"

"*Nee*. Not yet. But I haven't been watching that long."

Amanda stood at the window for a moment, her arms crossed over her chest. Her body shook.

"If you're cold you should *geh* back to bed," Bekah said.

Amanda shook her head, shifting from one bare foot to another. "*Nee*. If you're going to watch, so am I."

"Got your interest up?" Bekah grinned.

Her cousin didn't smile back, but she said, "*Ya*. A little"

They stood there in front of the window for a while, without talking. A light shone in the front window of the house, but other than that there were no signs of life. Finally the light went out, and Bekah wondered if he would come outside now. She waited awhile longer, and he didn't.

"He's not coming out tonight." Amanda yawned. "It's late; I'm going back to bed."

"I'll be there in a minute."

"Okay." Amanda hurried to the bed and slid beneath the covers, pulling them up to her chin. Bekah noticed she was still sleeping with the afghan Katherine had made.

Bekah waited a short while; then she also gave up. She had no idea what time it was, but it was late, and she had to get up early for school tomorrow. She had just moved away from the window when she thought she saw a shadow moving near the side of the old man's house. She held her breath. Was she going to catch him in the act again?

Then the shadow moved away and into the moonlight. It was just Roscoe. He seemed to be as fascinated with the old man's house as Bekah was. Roscoe barked at the house once, then trotted away. Bekah sighed. She pulled down the window and got into bed. It wasn't long before she went to sleep.

The next morning Bekah was dragging. For the first time, Amanda actually walked faster to school than she did. Bekah stifled a yawn as she walked into the school and took her seat in the back of the classroom.

As *Fraulein* Byler handed out graded papers, Bekah glanced at the older boys' table. Jacob wasn't there, and Bekah wondered if he might have been sick. But then she thought he might have skipped class. He had done so before, but none of the boys ever told on him. Bekah had a feeling *Fraulein* Byler knew Jacob wasn't missing school because he was ill, but because he was sneaking off. As she neared the back of the classroom, Bekah caught her teacher looking at Jacob's empty seat, sadness in her eyes.

Now the teacher was putting math problems on the blackboard. Bekah tried to focus, but her eyes kept closing. She leaned her head on her hand, staring at the division problems in front of her. She hated division, especially remainders. As the numbers blurred, she fought to stay awake.

"Rebekah Yoder!"

She popped up, her eyes wide. She looked up in the stern face of *Fraulein* Byler, standing right in front of her.

"Were you sleeping, Rebekah?"

Bekah started to shake her head, but she couldn't lie. "*Ya*, Fraulein. I was. I'm sorry."

"There will be no sleeping in this classroom. If you're tired, I suggest an earlier bedtime."

Bekah thought *Fraulein* Byler might give her an extra assignment for breaking the classroom rules, but she didn't. Instead, she turned around and headed to the front of the classroom to help another student with an assignment. Bekah breathed a sigh of relief.

She heard a snicker and cast a sideways glance at the table where Caleb and the older boys sat. Caleb grinned, and she knew he was the one who'd been laughing at her. She glared at him, then turned away, fully awake now and determined to conquer long division. She wasn't about to give Caleb Mullet the satisfaction of seeing her get in trouble again.

After the math lessons, it was time for lunch. Bekah met Ester and Miriam under the tree as she usually did. Miriam didn't look at her, turning her body more toward Ester. Bekah thought about asking her what her problem was, but she didn't. She was too tired to deal with Miriam today. She didn't open her lunch box right away. Instead, she let out another yawn. She wanted to stay up late again tonight, but she wasn't sure she could, not if she was going to be so tired the next day . . .

"Bekah? Bekah."

She turned at the sound of Ester's voice. "What?"

Her friend rolled her eyes. "You haven't heard a word we've said, have you?"

Bekah could feel her face heat up. "*Nee*. Sorry, I was thinking about something else." She met Miriam's gaze and saw the knowing glint in her eye. Oh, how she wished she hadn't said anything to her friend about the old man. But Miriam was one of her oldest friends; if anyone could keep a secret, Miriam could—although she sure had been acting strangely lately.

Bekah put all that out of her mind and focused on her friends before Ester became suspicious and started asking questions. She opened her lunch box and took out her sandwich, taking off the paper napkin it was wrapped in. Ham today. Her stomach growled, and she took a bite. "What were you all talking about?" she said around a mouthful of sandwich.

"Your cousin, actually." As Ester unpeeled a banana, she tilted her head in the direction of Amanda, who was seated near the entrance of the school. "I thought she'd join us again today. It's been nice having lunch with her lately. But today she seemed more quiet than usual."

Bekah searched her mind to come up with a valid excuse. Was Amanda thinking about the old man too? Was that why she was eating by herself? Or was she thinking about her mother? Either way, Bekah wouldn't betray Amanda. "She's just shy, remember?"

"So's Clara Fisher, but you don't see her sitting off by herself," Miriam said.

Bekah glanced at the small group of fifth and sixth graders sitting in a circle a few feet away from Amanda. Those girls were Amanda's age, and Bekah wished they would invite Amanda to join them. But what would be the point? It wasn't as if her cousin would say yes.

Ester finished her banana, neatly folding the peel and putting it in the plastic bag her sandwich came in. "Well, I'm going to *geh* talk to her. I don't think anyone should have to eat lunch alone."

"Even if it's her choice?" Miriam asked.

"Why would anyone choose to be alone if she can be with others?" Ester spun around and walked across the schoolyard. When she reached Amanda, she sat next to her.

Bekah was pleased that her friend was taking such an interest in Amanda. It was nice that Ester wasn't giving up on Amanda either.

Miriam leaned forward. "I'm kinda glad she left."

Bekah looked at her, her sandwich halfway to her mouth. "Why would you say that?"

"It's not that I don't want her around us. I do."

"Then why would you want her to leave? And why are you so mad at me?"

Miriam's eyebrows shot up. "Mad at you? I'm not mad at you."

"You ignored me at church yesterday."

"Oh, that." Miriam waved her hand. "I wasn't ignoring you."

"Sure seemed like it to me."

"Well, I'm not mad at you, okay?" She scooted closer to Bekah.

Bekah had to admit her friend didn't seem mad, at least not right now. Ugh. Why was everyone acting so weird lately?

Miriam lowered her voice. "I've been wanting to ask you all day—is there anything new going on with your neighbor?"

Bekah took a bite, taking her time to figure out what to say. Again she regretted saying anything to Miriam, because now she would have to answer questions she really didn't want to answer. "*Nee*," she said quietly, which was at least the partial truth. There wasn't anything new to report, unless you counted the old man yelling at her and Amanda. And she wasn't about to tell Miriam about that.

Miriam frowned. "That's too bad. Your mysterious neighbor is the most exciting thing to happen around here in weeks."

"What about a truck going through the school? That was pretty exciting."

"*Ya*, but we weren't here to see it." Miriam sounded disappointed. "Now everything's back to normal and *soooo* boring. I'm tired of school and it's only the second week. Oh wow—look who's coming over here."

Bekah glanced up, her mouth dropping open as she saw Ester and Amanda walking toward them. Ester's smile stretched across her face. "Amanda's decided to join us."

Amanda sat down next to Bekah, but she didn't say anything. She opened her lunch box and pulled out a cookie, breaking it in half. "Anyone want some?"

"Oh, me." Miriam reached out and took the half before anyone could answer. "I love *Frau* Yoder's cookies."

A baseball suddenly rolled near Bekah's foot. She picked it up. There were grass stains and dirt smudges all over it. At least it hadn't hit her this time. She looked over her shoulder to see Caleb running toward her. Oh boy. Why couldn't Melvin or one of the other boys come over here to retrieve it?

"Here comes Caleb," Miriam announced, a huge grin on her face.

Bekah looked at her, arching a brow. Great, her friend still had a crush on the biggest pain in Middlefield. "Sorry." He bent down and picked up the ball, then ran back over to the game.

"Isn't he wonderful?" Miriam pulled her knees to her chest and rested her chin on them. Her skirt hid her legs from view.

"He's a pest." Bekah grabbed her cookie out of her lunch box and started to take a bite. Then remembering Amanda's generosity, she broke hers in half and handed it to Ester.

"Danki," Ester said. She took a bite and looked at Amanda. "Do you like to cook?"

Amanda hesitated, then nodded slowly, still nibbling on the cookie half. Bekah wondered if she'd even bothered to eat her sandwich. She resisted the urge to check inside Amanda's lunch box. *"Ya*. I do. Sometimes."

"She helped me with apple pie the other night. It was delicious."

"I used to cook with my mother."

"Oh?" Ester polished off the cookie. "Where is she now?"

Amanda froze mid-chew, and Bekah wanted more than anything to rescue her from the question. But to do so would reveal that she knew about Amanda's mom, so she couldn't do that. Instead she sat there, helpless while Amanda tried to formulate an answer.

Finally she said, "Back in Paradise."

"Oh. I thought she might be somewhere else, since you said you used to cook with her."

Just then, *Fraulein* Byler called everyone to come back inside, and Bekah was grateful for the interruption. While Ester and Miriam headed for the *schulhaus*, she waited while Amanda put everything back into her lunch box. When her cousin stood up, Bekah said, "I'm glad you had lunch with us again today. It's nice when you join us."

Amanda looked at her, and for the first time Bekah saw something other than sorrow in her green eyes. "*Danki*. I am glad too."

After school let out, Bekah and Amanda started for home. They had only gone a few yards down the road when Bekah heard Caleb call out her name.

"Hey, Bekah! Wait up!"

Bekah groaned. "What does *he* want?"

"I don't know why you get so mad at him," Amanda said. "He seems nice to me."

"You mean except for the time he lied to you about the neighbor's *haus* being haunted?"

"You told me he was joking."

"Amanda, trust me. He seems nice to everyone, but that's because he doesn't play jokes on them or embarrass them like he does me."

"You said he likes to rile you up. Maybe if you didn't show him how mad you got, he'd leave you alone."

"I doubt it."

"Bekah!"

She turned to see Caleb running toward her. He was fast, and since he wasn't carrying any books and she was, there was no way she could outrun him. She had no choice but to slow down and wait for him. When he caught up, he was hardly out of breath.

"Can I talk to you for a minute?" he asked.

Bekah's brow lifted. She scanned his face, trying to see underneath his serious expression. She couldn't, and she wondered what was going on. "Sure," she answered.

He looked at Amanda. "Alone."

Amanda glanced from Bekah to Caleb, then back at Bekah. "I'll meet you at home," she said, speeding up.

"You don't have to—"

Caleb put his hand on Bekah's shoulder "Let her *geh* on ahead. You can catch up with her in a minute."

Bekah was relieved that whatever Caleb had to say would be short. "What do you want?"

"Why didn't you tell me the old man was back and moved in? And that he was digging in the yard?"

Bekah's mouth dropped open. "Who told you that?"

Caleb's gaze flitted to Amanda, who was several feet in front of them. Then he looked back at Bekah.

Bekah was shocked. She couldn't believe Amanda would betray her like this! Or had Miriam said something? Bekah couldn't believe that either. She had known Miriam all her life, and she trusted her. No, it must have been Amanda. She was family, but she had also been mad at Bekah for making her throw the Frisbee—and she hadn't wanted much to do with Bekah anyway. Was this Amanda's way of getting back at her? Not only had she broken a promise, she'd told Caleb—the last person on earth Bekah wanted to know! The more she thought about it, the more possible it sounded.

"Bekah, are you listening to me?"

His words jerked her out of her thoughts. "I want to know who told you, Caleb."

"It doesn't matter who told me," Caleb said. "I can't believe you didn't let me know!"

"Why would I? He's *my* neighbor."

"*Ya*, but you knew I was curious about what was going on at that *haus*. What else has he been doing?"

"I don't know, I haven't seen him do anything . . . well, except that one time. I just assumed he had been digging again because there were a few more covered holes in the yard."

"I knew it! I'm coming over there today."

Bekah shook her head. "Oh no, you're not. You know you're not supposed to come over to my *haus* by yourself anymore. That's *mei mami*'s rule, and I'm not breaking it. Neither are you."

"Fine, I'll wait for Johnny to take me."

Katherine was off work today, and Bekah knew her sister would love that idea, because it would give her a chance to see Johnny again. But Bekah wasn't the least bit thrilled. "Why don't you just mind your own business for once?"

"And why don't you stop being so selfish?"

"I'm being selfish?"

"*Ya.*" Caleb gave her a piercing look. "You're keeping this mystery all to yourself. That isn't fair."

"Your badgering me about it isn't fair. Look, there's no mystery." She almost bit her tongue on the lie, but she had to get rid of Caleb one way or another.

"You're a bad liar. I know there's something going on. Why won't you tell me?"

Bekah was fuming. They were coming up on Caleb's house. At least now she would be rid of him, so she could stew about Amanda. She had thought she could trust her cousin, but obviously she couldn't. And here she had kept the secret about Amanda's mother too!

"Bekah, wait a minute."

She stopped and turned around. "What?"

Caleb tilted back his straw hat. "If I promise not to play any more tricks on you, will you tell me the truth?"

She blinked. For the first time he was admitting he had done some awful things to her. Well, not exactly admitted, but he was going in the right direction. She quickly weighed her options—freedom from his pestering or letting him in on her secret, which was suddenly not her secret anymore. The answer was easy, especially since she knew he wouldn't stop bugging her until he got his way. "You promise?"

"*Ya*. I do." He looked directly at her, his serious expression reminding her of when he hit her with the baseball in the shin a few days ago. She had thought he'd been genuine at the time, but he had proved her wrong. She couldn't be sure of anything anymore, she thought, and hesitated.

"Bekah, come on. I won't tell anyone else. And I'll leave you alone for the rest of the school year."

Now that was an offer she couldn't refuse. She looked and saw Amanda had gone way ahead of her. Good. She didn't want to talk to her right now anyway. "All right."

Caleb led her off the road and into his front yard. "Tell me."

Bekah told him about the old man moving in next door and about the fresh holes she and Amanda had found. "That's it. See, not really a big deal."

He kicked at a tuft of grass. "Wish there was some way we could find out for sure. What if he's burying bones or something?"

"I'm sure that's not it." She shook her head. "Look, Caleb, I have to *geh*. I kept up my end of the deal, you'd better keep up yours."

Caleb nodded. "I will."

Bekah started down the road toward her house, breaking into a run when she realized her mother might want to know why she was late. Amanda would probably tattle that she was at Caleb's house, and she would get in trouble again. Right before she got home she saw that Amanda was waiting for her at the end of the driveway. Bekah slowed down and stood in front of her, her anger returning.

"What did Caleb want?" Amanda asked.

"As if you don't know." Bekah caught her breath. She glared at her cousin. Amanda was a good actress; Bekah would give her that. She looked genuinely confused.

Amanda held up her hands. "I don't."

"You told him about the old man."

"I did not!"

"*Ya*, you did. Caleb was asking me about him, and about the holes. How else would he know about that if you hadn't told him?"

Amanda shook her head. "It wasn't me. I made a promise, and I don't break my promises."

Bekah crossed her arms. "I don't believe you."

Amanda's eyes suddenly narrowed. "I don't care if you do or not." She whirled around and headed for the house, leaving Bekah standing at the end of the driveway.

A niggle of doubt wound its way through her. What if her cousin were telling the truth? But if she were, then that meant Miriam, Bekah's oldest friend, had betrayed her. Either way, it hurt that her trust had been broken.

Suddenly she heard the old man's front door shut. She turned around to see him coming out of the house. He looked directly at her and glared; she could see the anger in his eyes.

She wasn't in his yard, so she didn't understand why he was so angry. But it didn't matter; he kept staring at her.

"Bekah!"

Her mother stood on the front porch. Bekah turned away from the old man and followed her mother into the house.

Fourteen

AMANDA LOOKED out the window of the bedroom she shared with Bekah. She watched as Bekah sat on the wooden swing set, gently swinging back and forth, occasionally twirling around. Her cousin looked deep in thought. Well, she wasn't the only one.

Amanda clenched her fists. Bekah had called her a liar a couple of hours ago, and they hadn't said anything to each other since. Amanda had said a few words to Katherine, who was home for supper that night, but other than that, the meal had been eaten in silence. No doubt her aunt and uncle were worried again, but Amanda couldn't help it. She wasn't about to talk to Bekah, who didn't believe her when she told the truth.

But as she watched Bekah downstairs, she felt a small urge to go down and join her, despite her anger. She was getting tired of being cooped up in this room, and she had to admit having lunch with Bekah's friends this afternoon had been better than eating by herself. Even going over into the old man's yard the other day had been the beginning of having fun together, although it was a little creepy. Still, she wasn't going to be around someone who thought she was a liar who broke her promises. She would never break a vow, ever. Her mother did that, not her.

She pulled herself away from the window and went over to the bed. She sat down, but didn't lie down and face the wall like she had been doing for the past couple of weeks. Leaning forward, she propped her chin on her cupped hands. She'd finished her homework before supper, and now she was bored, something she hadn't been since she'd arrived from Paradise. Before she'd been able to keep herself occupied by thinking about her mother, praying her father would come back, and vowing not to experience a moment's happiness here. But what did she have to show for all that? Her mother was still gone, her father hadn't come back, and she was still miserable.

At the sound of a knock on the door she lifted her head up. It couldn't be Bekah; her cousin didn't knock anymore. And she had just seen her aunt in the vegetable garden a few yards from the barn, picking over the zucchini, which were the last vegetables in the garden. "Come in."

The door opened, and Katherine entered. Her older cousin smiled, the freckles on her cheeks rising with the movement. "Mind if I talk to you for a minute?"

Amanda shrugged. She'd heard those words so many times lately. Even if she did mind all the intrusions, it wasn't as if her aunt or cousins would leave her alone. But she wasn't sure she wanted to be alone anymore.

Katherine walked in and sat next to her on the bed. She had a box with a flowered lid in her hands. She put it on her lap. "I thought you might like some stationery."

"Why would I want that?"

"To write to your *mami* and *daed*."

"Did Bekah tell you to give that to me?"

"*Nee. Mami* mentioned you were thinking about writing some letters, so I got the stationery from work. We have some nice patterns in the gift shop."

"I haven't decided if I'm going to."

"I'm sure they miss you and would like to hear from you."

Amanda glanced down at the braided rug on the floor. She dug her toes in between two of the multicolored rope braids. "My *daed* might." She didn't add that her mother probably didn't care at all.

Katherine frowned. "Don't you miss them?"

A lump formed in Amanda's throat. Of course she missed them. She also missed Paradise. Middlefield was starting to grow on her, but it wasn't home. She missed her horse and her Paw-Paw. She also missed her father. But most of all she missed her mother. And she was mad at her too. Why did she have to leave? If she hadn't, Amanda would be back home, at her own school, teasing Paw-Paw with her favorite ball of yarn.

Above everything, she didn't understand why God hadn't heard her prayers. She had been taught all her life that God was an important part of her life, that she should pray to him and tell him all her problems. And she had done that, over and over. Still no answer. How was she supposed to believe in a God who listened to everyone but her?

"Well, I'll just leave this here for you, if you change your mind." Katherine set it on the other side of the bed. "Also, that offer to teach you how to crochet still stands. I'd love to show you how to make a scarf. You could wear it this winter."

Amanda pressed her lips together. She wanted to learn to crochet. And sew. And to learn how to cook better. Her aunt and cousin were ready to show her all these things, but she wanted to learn from her mother, not from them. But she couldn't say that. Her cousins didn't know about her mother leaving, and she didn't want to hurt *Aenti* Margaret's feelings.

She looked at Katherine. Her cousin was nice. And Bekah could be too, when she wasn't accusing Amanda of lying. "*Danki*. I'll think about it."

Katherine's face fell a little bit. "All right. Let me know. I picked up an extra skein of yarn while I was in town the other day." Katherine rose from the bed.

Amanda shoved the guilt away. She never asked Katherine to buy yarn for her. Or for her aunt and uncle to take her in. Or to share Bekah's room. She didn't ask for any of this.

After Katherine left, Amanda got up and went to the window again. Bekah wasn't on the swing anymore. Amanda briefly wondered where she went. Then she remembered she wasn't supposed to care. Trouble was, it was becoming harder not to.

"Need any help, *Mami*?"

Her mother stood up and looked at her, putting her hands on her hips. She glanced around the garden, which had been picked over. Some of the plants, such as the tomatoes and cornstalks, had already started to turn brown. "I think I've got it all. God truly blessed us with his bounty this year. We'll have plenty of canned vegetables this winter."

Bekah nodded. "That's *gut*." A sigh slipped out.

Her mother frowned. "What's the matter, *dochder*?"

Bekah didn't answer her right away. She couldn't tell her mother about Amanda's big mouth, not without revealing more than she wanted to about the old man next door. "*Nix*. I guess I'm just a little tired." At least that was true.

"Then maybe you should *geh* to bed."

"Now? It's only seven thirty."

Her mother grinned. "I knew you'd never agree to that." She picked up the basket, putting her arm through the handle. "You could see if Amanda wants to come outside. It's a beautiful evening. Your father and I are going for a walk a little later on. Both of you are welcome to join us."

Bekah shook her head. "Not tonight. Maybe some other time."

"Okay." She turned and faced Bekah. "Are you all right?"

"*Ya*? Why?"

"You were very quiet at supper tonight. I expect that from Amanda, but not from you. Did everything *geh* okay at school today?"

"Everything is fine. Like I said, I'm just a little tired."

Her mother cupped Bekah's chin with her free hand. "As long as it's nothing else. You would tell me, *ya*?"

Bekah swallowed. "*Ya*."

Her mother smiled, released her chin, and went back to the house.

Bekah watched her go, frowning. Then she heard a bark and turned to see Roscoe running toward her from next door. Her mood instantly lightened. At least Roscoe wouldn't ask her a bunch of questions or betray her trust. She really needed him right now.

Bekah met the dog at the edge of her yard. She knelt down, and it was then when she saw he had something in his mouth. "What's this?"

Roscoe put the object down in front of her. Then he sat on his haunches and looked at her, his tongue lolling out of his mouth. He barked once, then laid down, his nose pointed at what he had brought Bekah.

Bekah picked it up. It was a bone, not much bigger than her finger. A shiver ran through her. Surely he hadn't dug this up from the old man's yard? And if he had, it was probably an old steak bone or something, right? It couldn't be human. That was too creepy to think about.

Bekah examined the bone. It was dark and thin, with a joint at one end and pointed at the other, as if it had been broken off. She looked down at Roscoe. His muzzle resting against the ground, he lifted his eyes to her, the irises darting back and forth.

"You're not gonna tell me anything, are you?" She reached out and scratched behind his ears, something he always enjoyed. She looked at the bone again, then back at the yard. *What if . . . ?*

She shook her head as she shuddered again. Roscoe suddenly jumped up and darted off, which wasn't unusual for him. But she wished he'd stayed. She felt safer with him around.

Opening her palm, she glanced at the bone lying there. She should get rid of the nasty thing. But she couldn't bring herself to throw it away. What if she needed it later, like for . . . evidence? That's what Nancy Drew would do. She looked around her own backyard and considered where she could hide it. If it were out in the open, some animal, maybe even Roscoe, would cart it off. Then she spied the barn and realized she had the perfect hiding place.

Bekah went inside the barn and found a small shovel. She went to the back of the barn and started digging near the wall. When she had dug a shallow hole, she dropped the bone inside and covered it with the loose dirt. She packed it down, then stood back, marveling at how similar her hole looked to the ones she'd found in the old man's yard. Then she went back to the house. Maybe she'd read some more, see what Nancy was up to.

That night Bekah couldn't sleep. As usual, Amanda had fallen asleep before her, and for once Bekah was glad. She still wasn't ready to talk to her, although she wasn't as angry; she knew she'd have to forgive her cousin eventually. It was the Amish way to forgive, but it wasn't always easy.

After tossing and turning for a long time, Bekah got out of bed and looked out the window again. She thought about the bone she'd buried, and for a moment thought about telling Caleb. He knew everything anyway. He'd probably love to find out something creepy, like burying a bone. But she wouldn't tell him anything else. She was looking forward to his leaving her alone.

She breathed in the cool evening air and heard the bullfrogs and crickets in the distance, filling the evening with their night music. Her gaze strayed to the old man's house. It was dark, and she figured he'd gone to bed already. But then she heard the squeak of a door opening. The full moonlight illuminated his backyard, and she saw him walking out of the house, shovel over his arm. Her heart started to pound.

I knew it! She was about to catch him in the act. Scary or not, she wished she could see what he was burying. He stood there with the shovel on his shoulder, walking around the tall grass at the back of the property and looking down at the ground, as if he were trying to find the perfect spot. Then he stopped looking and started to dig. And dig. And dig some more. He wasn't digging a small hole like the others. He was scooping out mound after mound of dirt. Bekah watched, fascinated. What in the world was he going to do with a such a big hole?

She glanced over her shoulder at Amanda's sleeping form. How she wished she could wake up her cousin and show her what the old man was doing! But she couldn't, not unless she wanted the news broadcast all over the schoolyard on Monday morning. She went back to watching the man dig.

It seemed like forever, but he finally stopped digging, leaning on the handle of his shovel. He wiped the top of his bald head with the back of his hand, then let the shovel drop. He walked back to the house and went inside.

Bekah waited for a long time, so long she wondered if he'd ever come back out. Finally he did, carrying what looked like a large box. Or a chest. Excitement churned within her. Was he burying some kind of treasure? That was more exciting, and pleasant, than bones. He piled the dirt back in the hole, then tamped it down. He trudged to the house and leaned the shovel against the wall, then went back inside.

A cloud passed over, covering the sky in darkness. Bekah went back to bed and pulled her quilt to her chin, her mind whirring. She'd never get to sleep tonight.

The rest of the week passed quietly. Too quietly—her cousin gave Amanda the silent treatment. But at least Bekah wasn't still accusing her of things she hadn't done, and she didn't say anything when Amanda began to eat lunch with her and Ester and Miriam. Amanda thought maybe it was because Bekah was so tired—she was always yawning, and *Fraulein* Byer had even asked if she were getting enough sleep—but even though Amanda suspected Bekah was staying up late spying on the old man, she said nothing. On

Friday, after supper, the two girls had even sat on the porch together with Roscoe.

On Saturday morning Amanda woke up before everyone else. The sun hadn't even come up yet. She snuck out of bed and crept downstairs; the entire house was quiet. She opened the back door, crossed the deck, and stepped into the yard. Cold dew covered her bare feet as she walked in the grass and sat down on the damp swing. She didn't care that her nightgown was getting wet, or that she was growing cold. She had to get out of that house, and away from the nightmare that had plagued her last night.

Her mother had appeared in the dream, holding her arms out to Amanda. But no matter how fast Amanda ran toward her, her mother moved farther and farther away. Through her tears, she had dashed toward her mother, only to have her disappear completely. Even now she could hear her mother calling her name as she vanished into darkness.

Amanda wrapped her arms around her shoulders, trying to shake the dream from her mind. She tucked her chin against her chest, listening to the sparse twitters of the early birds. She should go inside where it was warmer. But she wasn't ready. The coldness helped clear her mind.

Then she heard a squeaking sound coming from next door. She peered into the darkness, barely able to make out a shadowy form coming out of the house. Amanda froze, not wanting to let him know she was there. He grabbed something—probably the shovel—leaning against the house, then walked to the edge of the yard that bordered her aunt and uncle's property.

Amanda held her breath, digging her toes into the cold, clammy dirt underneath the swing.

Sure enough, he started to dig. Bekah had been right—he was digging in his yard! But why? The old man quickly finished digging a small hole, then dropped the shovel. The sky suddenly pinked, and Amanda could see him reaching in his pocket and pulling something out. He dropped it into the hole and covered it with dirt. Then he picked up the shovel, leaned it against the house, and walked back inside.

She let out a long breath when he shut the door. She wondered what he had dropped in that hole. She should tell Bekah about it. But then she remembered that Bekah had called her a liar, and she changed her mind. She hopped out of the swing and went back inside. She entered the kitchen, then stopped when she saw her aunt standing in front of the gas stove, lighting it with a match.

"You're up early for a Saturday." Her aunt shook out the match and laid it on the counter next to the stove. She put a teakettle over the flame. "Have trouble sleeping?"

Amanda thought to tell her no, but changed her mind. "A little."

"Anything in particular keeping you up?"

"Nothing I can't handle."

"Oh, I know you can handle it." Her aunt looked at her and smiled. She didn't have her white *kapp* on this morning.

A bright blue kerchief covered her light brown hair, and she wore a blue dress, one shade darker than her head covering. "I just wanted you to know I'm here if you need to talk about anything."

Her aunt had said that more than once, and Amanda always just shook her head politely and said she'd think about it. She was about to respond the same way, but then she thought about the man digging in his yard. Her aunt would probably want to know about that. But she held her tongue, remembering her promise to Bekah. Even though Bekah thought she'd already told their secret, she hadn't, and she wouldn't go back on her word.

Aenti Margaret went to the pantry on the other side of the kitchen and pulled out a loaf of bread. "Would you mind getting the milk and eggs from the cooler?" she asked. "I think we'll have French toast this morning."

Amanda nodded and went to the basement where the Yoders kept a large white cooler. Like many Amish who didn't use electricity, Bekah's family stored the food that needed to be kept cold in a cooler during the warm months, and kept the cooler outside during the winter, where the food stayed naturally cold. She got the food and went back upstairs, handing the ingredients to her aunt.

"Usually Bekah's up by now. She likes to help me make French toast." Her aunt looked at her. "Would you like to help me instead? I don't think it would hurt to let Bekah sleep in a little bit."

Amanda hesitated. Normally, she would have said no,

but . . . she found she really wanted to help her aunt. "*Ya*," she said.

Aenti Margaret smiled. "*Wunderbaar*. I can teach you my mother's secret recipe."

For the next thirty minutes, Amanda and *Aenti* Margaret worked in the kitchen. Turned out the secret recipe was really just a secret ingredient: vanilla in the egg-and-milk mixture. Amanda had dipped the last slice of bread in the remaining mixture when Bekah came in. Like her mother, she wore a kerchief over her head, this one pale green.

She looked at them with sleepy eyes. "You made breakfast without me?"

"I thought you would like to sleep in a little bit. You've seemed tired lately." *Aenti* Margaret put the last plate on the table.

"But you know I love to make French toast," Bekah said.

"I know, *dochder*. But you'll have lots of chances to help me in the kitchen."

Bekah looked at Amanda, anger flitting in her eyes. Amanda glanced away, focusing on the French toast frying in the pan in front of her. So her cousin was still mad at her. That wasn't her fault or her problem. Still, she couldn't help but feel bad that she and Bekah were on the outs. She didn't realize how much she missed Bekah until her cousin had stopped speaking to her. Ever since she'd arrived here, she'd wanted to be left alone. Now that Bekah was actually doing that, Amanda didn't like it much at all.

A car horn honked outside. Amanda glanced out the

kitchen window and saw a small, gray, four-door car in the driveway. A few seconds later Katherine burst into the kitchen, still pinning her *kapp* to her hair.

"Sorry, *Mami*, I don't have time for breakfast. I'm working the morning shift at the restaurant and I'm running late." Katherine didn't stop, flying out the kitchen door to catch her ride. "See you later!" she yelled from outside.

Aenti Margaret shook her head, chuckling. "They sure work Katherine a lot of hours. I rarely see her anymore." She looked at Amanda. "I guess it's just the four of us. Bekah, please see what's keeping your father. He went to the barn awhile ago to take care of Sparky. Let him know it's time to eat."

Bekah nodded, but didn't look at Amanda. She left the kitchen.

"I think it's ready to flip over." *Aenti* Margaret handed Amanda the spatula. "You don't want it to burn around the edges. That can happen easily."

Amanda nodded. It felt good to be helpful. For a moment she could pretend that she was in her own kitchen, her mother giving her instructions on cooking instead of her *aenti*. She couldn't have that, not now at least. But while she was here, maybe she should do what her aunt and uncle had been encouraging her to do—be a part of their family.

Fifteen

BEKAH WENT out to the barn and found her father there, pitching hay into Sparky's stall. He looked up as Bekah walked in. He smiled. "Breakfast ready?"

"*Ya*. Do you need some help?" She looked around to see that her father had straightened up the barn.

"Well, if you had come out here a few minutes ago, I could have used your help to clean out Sparky's stall. But it's already done." He pitched one more pitchfork full of hay over the top of her stall.

"You cleaned out her stall this morning?" Usually he saved that task for Saturday afternoon.

"*Ya*. Didn't your mother tell you?" He put the tines of the pitchfork against the dirt floor of the barn and leaned against the handle. "We're going to town today. Your *mami* has some shopping to do, and I'm going to stop at that new buggy shop over on Hayes Road. Kine's, I think the name is. Our buggy's going to need a new wheel pretty soon, and I want to check out his prices."

"So you're going to be gone all day?"

"Most of it." He hung the pitchfork next to the rest of the lawn tools, which were hanging on a long pegboard nailed to the barn wall. He turned and looked at Bekah. "Your *mami* and I expect you and Amanda to behave yourselves while we're gone."

"We will." She hid her irritation. She was thirteen years old. Of course she would behave herself.

"And under no circumstances are you to go next door. I don't want you bothering Mr. Harvey."

Bekah's brow lifted. So that was his name. "Have you talked to him?"

"Only briefly." Her father removed his hat and shoved a thick hand through his reddish-brown hair. "He likes to keep to himself, and he has that right. So respect his privacy and stay in our yard only. You have no business being over there anyway."

Bekah wished she could ask her father more questions about Mr. Harvey, but she didn't want to raise his suspicions by being too interested in their neighbor—in spite of her reputation for being nosy. "When are you leaving?"

"Right after breakfast. Which we better *geh* eat before your mother gets upset with me."

Bekah and her father walked back from the barn and entered the kitchen. The aroma of sweet French toast and maple syrup filled the air. Amanda and her mother were already seated at the table. Bekah and her father went to wash their hands. After they all sat down and said grace, her father spoke. "Margaret, I told Bekah about us leaving this morning."

"And I filled Amanda in." Her mother poured syrup over a thick slice of French toast.

"Did you remind her about staying away from Mr. Harvey's *haus*?"

"I did, *ya*." Amanda looked at Bekah's father and nodded.

"*Gut*."

Her mother looked at *Daed* for a moment. "Thomas, I wonder if we should make more of an effort with Mr. Harvey."

"What do you mean?" He crammed a large forkful of toast in his mouth.

"We could *geh* over there as a family, formally introduce ourselves. Bring him a few cookies and welcome him to the neighborhood."

"I don't think that's a *gut* idea, Margaret. I was just telling Bekah that he likes to keep to himself."

"But maybe he would be friendlier if we were friendlier to him."

Her father looked at her mother, a small smile on his face. "That's nice of you, Margaret, but I think it would be a waste of time. Some folks don't like people. That's just how they are, *ya*? I think he bought the Harper place because he wanted to get away from people."

"But we're people, *Daed*," Bekah said.

"I know, but there are only a couple of *hauss* on our street, and no neighbors behind us. We're pretty isolated. Mr. Harvey seems to like that just fine."

Bekah looked at her mother, who still seemed unsure. "But—"

"Margaret," *Daed* said gently, but in a firm tone, "I'm right about this."

Her mother nodded and picked up her fork again. "Amanda, Katherine says she would like to teach you how to crochet. Would you like me to pick up some yarn for you in town?"

Amanda shook her head. Bekah noticed her cousin had eaten every bit of her French toast, which was a first. "*Danki*, *Aenti* Margaret, but Katherine already has yarn. We don't need anymore."

"All right."

Bekah waited for her mother to ask her if she needed anything, and when she didn't, she felt a pinch of jealousy. She couldn't believe she was jealous of her cousin getting attention, especially since she understood why. Still, she couldn't help it. She looked at Amanda, who was drinking her milk. Bekah wasn't as upset with her as she had been the day before, and she was close to being able to forgive her. But she wasn't quite there yet.

Her father pushed away from the table. "I'll *geh* hitch up Sparky. What time will you be ready, Margaret?"

"In a few minutes. I need to clean up the kitchen and finish getting dressed; then I'll be ready."

"I'll get the kitchen, *Aenti* Margaret," Amanda piped up.

"You will?" Her mother looked as surprised as Bekah felt. Her cousin hadn't offered to do anything since she'd arrived from Paradise. Amanda had complied with any chore Bekah's parents gave her, but this was the first time she had volunteered to do anything.

"That would be great. Bekah can help you."

Bekah hid a scowl. She didn't want to help Amanda, but now she had no choice.

Her mother left, and the girls picked up the dishes. Bekah ran water in the sink, while Amanda cleared the rest of the table.

"I'll wash, you dry," Bekah said.

"Fine."

The girls did the dishes in silence. Bekah handed Amanda the plates, glancing at her cousin every once in a while. As the silence stretched on, she felt more and more uncomfortable. But she couldn't bring herself to say anything.

They finished the dishes just as her mother came out. Amanda had grabbed the wet dishrag and was wiping the table when her mother walked into the kitchen. "Your *vatter's* out there waiting on me," she said. "We should be back later this afternoon." Her mother pinned her black shawl around her neck. She had already put on her black bonnet, which fit over her white *kapp*. "If there is an emergency, use the cell phone in the barn."

Bekah nodded. "We'll be fine, *Mami*. Don't worry." Bekah had stayed by herself plenty of times, and had also stayed with Katherine, and before that, their older sister Leah, and never once had they had to use the cell phone.

Her mother smiled. "All right. See you later."

Bekah and Amanda both followed her outside. Bekah watched from the back porch as her parents climbed in the buggy. They both waved good-bye as Sparky cantered down the driveway and out to the main road.

The girls stood there for a moment. Then Amanda turned around without saying anything and went inside. Bekah sighed. This was silly. She should go inside and talk to her. She was about to do that when she heard a car door slam. She walked to the edge of the house and peeked around the corner, just in time to see Mr. Harvey back his minivan out of the driveway.

She forgot about Amanda as an idea came to her—this was her chance to check out what the old man had been digging in his backyard. Of course, she shouldn't go over there; her parents' warning reverberated in her ears. To do so would be a blatant disregard for their rules. But . . . when else was she going to have a chance to find out what he was burying in the backyard? With both him and her parents gone, she could easily sneak over there and quickly unearth one hole, then cover it back up. Still, she couldn't rid herself of the guilt she felt just thinking about disobeying her parents.

She began to pace, the cool grass threading in and out between her toes as she walked. She argued with herself, deciding one minute to go next door and the next to mind her parents and stay put. If only she knew what to do. She halted her steps and looked at the grass in his backyard. It wasn't overgrown yet, but he had moved in two weeks ago; it looked pretty shaggy.

Then she heard a dog bark and saw Roscoe trotting her way. She grinned. A sign, it had to be. Why else would Roscoe, who was an expert digger, show up? She waited for the dog to approach, then knelt down and petted him for a moment. "You want to help me dig for treasure?"

Amanda was bored. After leaving Bekah she had gone into the living room and tried to read one of the books in the pile by the end table, but she couldn't get into the story. She kept thinking about Bekah outside. She couldn't believe it, but for once she felt like playing. Even Frisbee, an activity she didn't like very much, sounded appealing right now. But Bekah wasn't speaking to her. For a short while Amanda considered going out there and telling Bekah she was sorry, even though she hadn't done anything wrong. Bekah would at least talk to her then. But she couldn't bring herself to do it. Instead, she put the book back and went upstairs.

She saw the stationery box Katherine had brought to her the other day. Maybe she should write her father. But what would she say? She didn't dare ask about her mother, afraid of the answer she might get. She also didn't dare ask when he might come get her. She'd been here for nearly a month now, and she hadn't heard anything from him.

Irritation rose inside her. Why should she bother to write him if he couldn't take the time to send her even a little note, or even call *Onkel* Thomas on his cell phone to check on her?

Turning her back on the stationery, she went to the window and looked outside. It was a beautiful, cloudless day, the sun shining bright in the sky, the temperature perfect. Her gaze went to the old swing set in the middle of the yard. She wanted to swing, to be outside enjoying the day. Why should she let Bekah or her parents ruin her mood? She had spent enough time feeling sorry for herself.

She started to move away from the window when she noticed a flash of movement next door. She peered out the window, wondering if she imagined what she saw. Sure enough, Bekah was in the backyard, Roscoe sitting next to her. She was kneeling on the ground, hunched over. Amanda instantly knew what she was doing. How could she disobey her parents like that?

Amanda ran downstairs and out the door, rushing into Mr. Harvey's yard. "What are you doing?"

Bekah's head shot up and she groaned. "You better not tell on me again."

"For the last time, I didn't say anything about this." Amanda looked down on the ground to see what Bekah was doing.

Her cousin stood up and went to her. "*Geh* back home."

"Not until I see what you found out."

"I haven't found anything, so you can *geh* back."

Amanda tried to sidestep Bekah, but with every move she made Bekah blocked it. "Now who's not telling the truth?" Amanda said. "You did find something."

"Even if I did, I wouldn't show you."

Frustrated, Amanda threw up her hands. "Fine. *Geh* ahead and be that way. But you're going to get in trouble if you get caught."

"The only way I'm going to get caught is if you say something."

Amanda crossed her arms. "Maybe I will. It would serve you right for disobeying *Aenti* Margaret and *Onkel* Thomas."

"Then you'll get in as much trouble because you're here too."

"Only because you're over here."

Roscoe barked. It was as if he wanted them to stop arguing. Amanda knelt down, and Roscoe came to her. "Hey, *bu*," she said. She petted the top of his head. His fur was soft. He licked her cheek. She chuckled, some of her frustration with Bekah disappearing. She looked up at her cousin. "Bekah, I don't want to fight with you anymore."

Bekah's scowl relaxed a bit. "I don't want to fight with you either." She sighed, her shoulders slumping. "I forgive you for telling Caleb about Mr. Harvey."

"But I didn't tell him. Honest."

"You're the only one who knew about it."

"You didn't tell anyone else?"

Bekah paused, then shook her head, glancing away. "*Nee*."

Amanda stood up. Roscoe sat down near her feet. The

grass in Mr. Harvey's yard reached his neck. "Maybe Caleb's been spying over here."

Bekah shook her head. "That's impossible. We would know."

"Did you ask him who told you?"

"*Ya*. He told me it didn't matter." Bekah shrugged her shoulders. "I guess I can ask him tomorrow at church. But that means I'd have to talk to him."

"He's not that bad."

"No, not since he promised he'd leave me alone if I told him everything." Bekah smiled.

"Did you?"

"*Ya*. That was an offer I couldn't refuse."

The girls chuckled. Amanda felt better than she had in weeks. She was glad Bekah wasn't mad at her anymore. She looked at the ground behind Bekah. "You really didn't find anything?"

"Not yet." Bekah went back to the hole. She knelt down and brushed back the grass. "I was just about to dig it up when you came over here."

"I still think this is a bad idea. What if Mr. Harvey comes back?"

"We'll hear his car coming down the road. We can run back home if we do, and he'll never know we were over here."

"What if he notices that we dug up the hole?"

Bekah pointed to Roscoe, who was sniffing at something in the grass a few feet away. "He'll think Roscoe did it." She looked at Amanda. "Do you want to know what's under here or not? We're wasting time talking about it."

Amanda hesitated, then nodded. Bekah started to dig, and Amanda put her hands in the dirt too. She felt the cold dirt sliding underneath her fingernails as she pulled away small clumps of it. They went down a few inches, then a few more.

Bekah frowned. "There's nothing here. That can't be right." She sat back on her feet. "I saw him digging out here last night. He put something in here, I just know it."

Amanda looked at the empty hole. "Maybe you're mistaken about him putting something in it."

"But that doesn't make any sense. Why dig a bunch of holes and fill them back in? Plus, I saw him dig a huge hole in the backyard. He put some kind of chest in it."

"Really? Are you sure?"

Bekah nodded. "We need to find that hole. C'mon, let's put this dirt back and look for it."

They quickly put the dirt back and patted it down. Amanda looked down at her black palms. She and Bekah got to their feet, and she followed Bekah to the back of the yard.

"It's got to be here somewhere." Bekah bent slightly at the waist, looking down at the ground. She parted the grass with her foot. "How hard can it be to find a big hole?"

Amanda thought the same thing, but as they searched they couldn't find it. The length of the grass made it difficult to see the ground, and the numerous bumps in the yard didn't help. The more time they spent looking, the more nervous Amanda became. "We have to find this soon, Bekah."

"I know, I know." She looked over her shoulder at Roscoe, who had left Mr. Harvey's yard and was sunning himself on the Yoder's driveway. "If only we had his nose."

"I know . . . wait." Amanda's big toe landed on something soft. "I think I found it."

Bekah came running over. "Where?"

"Right here." She knelt down and shoved the grass aside. It gave way easily, and Amanda pulled out a tuft with her hand. "I think this might be it."

Excitement entered Bekah's eyes. "I'm sure it is."

They started uncovering the dirt, but soon Amanda realized it wouldn't be as easy to unearth the large hole as it had the smaller one. "We need a shovel."

Bekah stood up. "Mr. Harvey had one leaning against the house, but it's gone." She glanced down at Amanda. "*Daed* has one in the barn. It's near Sparky's stall. *Geh* get it and I'll keep digging here."

"All right." Amanda stood up and ran to the barn. She searched for the shovel, but didn't see it right away. She knew her uncle kept his pitchfork, shovel, rake, and hoe hanging on a peg rack against the wall, and all the tools were there except for the shovel. Amanda continued to search the wall of the barn, hurrying because Mr. Harvey could come back any minute.

Sixteen

Bekah hurried, pulling dirt out of the ground, but trying to be careful as she did it. Mr. Harvey had dug this hole differently than the others. Not only was it bigger and deeper, but he had carefully covered it with the dirt and grass, which was why it had been so hard for her and Amanda to find. Now that they had, they couldn't waste any more time. Where was Amanda? She'd been gone longer than she should have. It didn't take that long to find a shovel.

It crossed Bekah's mind that her cousin might have changed her mind. Amanda hadn't been that eager to disobey Bekah's parents. Truth be told, Bekah didn't like doing it either. Sweat dripped from her face, and it wasn't only because she was warm from digging. Her stomach churned with a mix of excitement and guilt. She shouldn't be here. Yet she couldn't turn back now. Not when she was so close to finding out what was in the chest.

She kept digging. The hole was pretty deep, and still she

hadn't hit anything hard, just more dirt. But it was loose dirt, which made her believe she was in the right place. Any minute she would feel the top of the hard chest. She glanced up to see if Amanda was coming. She wasn't and Bekah noticed Roscoe had also disappeared.

Her arms grew tired and her hands ached. She let out a long breath and stopped. It was no use. Amanda wasn't coming back and she couldn't keep digging. She'd spent enough time in the yard—more than she should have. Mr. Harvey might show up, and then she would be in more trouble than she'd ever been in her life! Finding out what was in the chest wasn't worth that.

She got back on her knees and bent over, cupping her hands and picking up the dirt, putting it back in the hole. Her shoulders burned as she put the top tufts of grass back in place, patting them down. Wiping the sweat off her forehead with the back of her hand, she got up. Time to go home.

Then she felt a hand clamp over her mouth and an arm wrap around her shoulders. "You say one word, I'll break your neck."

After what seemed like forever, Amanda finally found the shovel, which wasn't in the barn at all, but leaning outside against the back wall. Bits of hay and horse dung clung to the end of it. Her uncle must have used the shovel and forgotten to put it back. She picked it up and ran over to Mr. Harvey's. But when she got there, Bekah was gone.

She ran to where they had been digging—all the grass and dirt had been replaced. Bekah must have given up and gone back inside. Which wasn't a bad idea. They shouldn't have been digging up Mr. Harvey's yard in the first place. Although she was still curious about what he had buried, she breathed a sigh of relief that they were giving up their quest. She couldn't stand the guilt.

She went back to the barn and hung up the shovel where it belonged. Then she noticed Sparky's stall door was open. Knowing the horse would be hungry and thirsty when she came back from town, she went to the corner of the barn where her uncle kept Sparky's feed. She scooped out the fine yellow grain and poured it into the horse's trough, then checked her water. Satisfied Sparky would be set when her aunt and uncle came back, she left the barn and went back inside.

"Bekah?" she called out as she entered the kitchen. When she didn't hear her cousin reply, Amanda went to the living room, then upstairs, expecting her to be in her room. She wasn't. She came back downstairs, thinking she was in the bathroom. But that room was empty too. Amanda frowned. "Bekah? Where are you?"

She dashed upstairs again, dread pooling inside her. She looked in Katherine's room, and Bekah's parents' room. She even went back to Bekah's room and checked inside her closet. "If this is a game, it isn't funny!" But Bekah didn't answer, and after a thorough search of the basement, it became clear that she wasn't in the house.

Amanda ran back outside to the barn, calling for Bekah the whole time. Her cousin wasn't in the barn, or behind it. She wasn't in the field past the house, by the pond, or in the front yard. Amanda went to the edge of the driveway and lifted her hand over her eyes, searching the field across the street for any sign of her cousin. But she didn't see anything.

She started to turn to go back to the house when she saw a car parked down the street, near Mr. Harvey's house but not directly in front of it. The dread that had been churning inside her turned to a cold knot in the pit of her stomach. How long had that car been there? It didn't seem right for it to be parked on the side of the road, next to another open field. She looked around, but didn't see anyone. Including Bekah.

Bekah's heart stopped as she felt herself dragged from the yard through the back door and into Mr. Harvey's house. She breathed in a musty odor, which made her sick to her stomach. The man's hand remained pressed against her mouth, and he was squeezing her tightly with his arm.

He took her into the kitchen, which was half the size of her kitchen at home. He pulled her against him, speaking low in her ear. "I'm gonna let you go now. You scream, it will be the last sound you ever make." He removed his hand from her mouth and spun her around to face him.

She gasped for air, frozen still. She recognized him immediately—it was the tattooed man, the scary man who had been at the house right before Mr. Harvey moved in.

Her eyes snapped to the tattoos on his arms. One was a skull and crossbones, covered partially by his black T-shirt. A dragon with flames rolling out of its mouth decorated his forearm. She looked at his face, noticing a tattoo of a tear at the corner of one of his eyes, which were wide and filled with rage. Terrified, she clenched her hands, automatically stepping back from him.

"Where are you goin', little girl?" His lips curled in a sneer. "You're not getting away from me, not until you tell me what I wanna know."

Bekah backed away as he drew closer, until her back was against the wall. He towered over her and leaned down. He smelled of cigarettes, and his breath reeked, like he'd been chewing on something rotten.

"I saw you digging around back there. Is that where the old man keeps the money?"

"What money?" Her voice shook.

"Don't act like you don't know what I'm talking about."

"I don't." Her voice rose. "I don't even know Mr. Harvey."

"You know his name. That's enough. So tell me where the money is."

She noticed the sweat forming on his upper lip. The house was stuffy and smelled weird, but it wasn't hot. The man started to pace, but instead of walking he was bounding back and forth, sliding across the kitchen floor. Then he came up to her. "Tell me where the money is. Now!"

The force of his voice brought tears to her eyes. Her body trembled. "I don't know."

He shoved a hand over his shorn hair. Then he grabbed her by the arm, his hand clamping over one of her prayer *kapp* ribbons. As he yanked her toward him, he pulled her *kapp* sideways, the bobby pins coming loose. He slammed her down in a chair. "Don't move!"

She couldn't have moved if she wanted to. Fear clawed at her, making her mouth numb and her hands ice cold. *Please, Lord, help me. I promise I'll never snoop again. Just send somebody here to save me!*

Amanda didn't know what to do. Fear for Bekah kept her in place, and her imagination started to take flight. What if someone had kidnapped her? Or worse? Then she calmed down. That was ridiculous. Kidnappings happened in books, not in real life, and not among the Amish. She had never heard of such a thing before. But she still didn't have an explanation for what happened to Bekah.

She thought about the cell phone in the barn. But who could she call? And what would she say? That her cousin disappeared? Would anyone even believe her? She only knew one number, and that was her father's. Like her *Onkel* Thomas, her *daed* kept a cell phone in his barn. But what could he do to help so many miles away?

She couldn't stand at the end of the driveway staring at that car, that much she knew. As she went back to the house, trying to figure out what to do, she looked at Mr. Harvey's house. Bekah wouldn't have gone in there, would she?

Would she have gone inside to look for a shovel? But that didn't make sense—who kept a shovel in the house?

Still, Amanda thought she should check and see before she called anyone. She walked toward the back of the house. Were those voices? She stopped, just underneath a window, and pressed herself to the side of the house.

"I don't even know Mr. Harvey."

Amanda's eyes grew wide. Bekah sounded terrified, and the man in there with her sounded crazy. She was almost too scared to move, but she had to. She had to do something to save Bekah.

"It's gotta be here somewhere." The man started yanking out the kitchen drawers, dumping the contents on the linoleum floor. There wasn't much to dump out, and some of the drawers were empty. The man threw the last drawer on the floor, spun around, and glared at Bekah. "Stop lying to me and tell me where the money is!"

She couldn't stop the tears from flowing. "I don't know."

"Stop cryin', or I'll give you something to cry about." He bent down and grabbed the back of her *kapp*, clutching the bun of hair she had pinned underneath. He pulled on it, hard.

She winced, but forced herself to stop crying. She could see the man was out of his mind. This close, she noticed his red-rimmed eyes and the dark shadows underneath.

He let go of her head and shoved her off the chair. "Get up."

She scrambled to her feet as he came at her again. "Now, one more time. Where. Is. The. Money?"

Her mouth opened, but she couldn't say a word. Thoughts raced through her mind as she tried to figure out what to tell him. He didn't want to hear the truth. "Out . . . side."

"That's what I thought." He grabbed her again, pinning her arm against her back. "You're comin' with me. And you're gonna show me where he buried the money. Got that?"

She nodded and heard her shoulder crack. She whimpered, which made the man pin her arm higher. He pushed her toward the door, then outside.

"Amanda, you've got to calm down. I don't understand anything you're saying."

Through tears Amanda tried to tell her father what was going on. She was calm as she dialed his number, but when she heard his voice, she broke down. "Bekah's . . . in . . . trouble."

"What kind of trouble? Where are *Aenti* Margaret and *Onkel* Thomas?"

"Not . . . here." Amanda forced herself to take a deep breath. She wasn't helping Bekah by being hysterical. "They're in Middlefield."

"Okay. Why don't you tell me about Bekah."

Her father's soothing voice helped calm Amanda down even more. She told her father about Mr. Harvey, about the holes, the buried chest, and finally about Bekah being held in the house. "Something bad is gonna happen to her, *Daed*. I don't know what to do."

Her father didn't say anything for a long moment. Then he finally spoke. "Amanda. I know you miss your *mamm* very much. I do too. But she's not ready to come back yet, and I can't come get you until she does. She just needs a little more time. But we're talking about it now, and I'm sure she'll come back home soon."

Amanda couldn't believe what she was hearing. "I'm not telling you this so you'll come get me. Bekah's in real trouble, *Daed*."

"So everything you told me is the truth?"

"I promise it is."

"Listen to me, Amanda." His tone turned from soothing to alarmed. "You need to call the police. Do you know how to do that?"

"Dial 911?"

"Right. Then you *geh* inside *Onkel* Thomas's *haus* and lock the doors. Wait until the police get there. Do not *geh* over to that *haus*. You can't help Bekah yourself. Do you understand?"

"*Ya*."

"All right. I'm hanging up now. Take the cell phone with you in the *haus*. I'll call you in five minutes."

Amanda hung up and did as her father said. She dialed 911, and the police took her seriously. They were sending someone right away. She was running back to Bekah's house when she saw the old man's back door open. Amanda wanted to stop, but didn't dare. She ran inside and locked the doors, like her father told her to. Then she dashed upstairs to Bekah's bedroom and went to the window.

The man was pushing Bekah out the back door. Bekah's face was pinched with pain. Amanda gripped the phone, wanting to call out to her. But that would make everything worse, so she stayed silent. The man and Bekah went over to the large hole she and Bekah had tried to dig out a short while ago. He shoved Bekah to the ground. Amanda could hear him shouting, but didn't understand what he was saying.

The phone rang, and Amanda immediately answered it. "Hello?" she whispered.

"Amanda, it's *Daed*. Are you in the *haus*?"

"*Ya*."

"Did you call the police like I told you to?"

"They're on their way."

"*Gut*, Amanda."

"*Daed*? I'm scared." Her palms grew slick as she held the phone and watched Bekah digging with one hand, the other lying limply at her side. What did that man do to her?

"I know, *lieb*. Just keep talking to me until the police get there."

"I will, *Daed*."

"There's one other thing you can do, Amanda."

She gripped the phone with both hands. "What?"

"Pray. Pray harder than you ever have in your life."

Seventeen

Pain seared Bekah's left arm as she scooped out dirt with her right. The black ribbons of her *kapp* dangled in her face as she dug in the dirt, the man standing directly over her. She could only use one hand. He had done something to her arm. Maybe broke it, she wasn't sure. Right now she was thankful he hadn't done something worse.

"You said it was here." He knelt down beside her. "You told me the money was here."

"I—I thought it was."

"You thought? Move!" He shoved her aside and started scratching at the dirt. "C'mon, c'mon! It has to be here!"

Bekah started to scoot away, but he snaked his arm out and grabbed her ankle. "Don't try that again."

She nodded, trying to keep herself from throwing up. She couldn't believe this was happening. What would he do if he found the money? Would he leave then? Would he let her go? She prayed he would, and prayed even harder he would find what he was looking for, and soon.

"It's not here." His hands and arms blurred as he dug harder. "It's not here." He stopped, his chest heaving. Then he looked at her. "You think you're funny, playin' a joke on me?"

"It's not a joke. I thought it was here, honest."

He lifted his hand toward her. "I'll teach you a lesson you'll never forget."

"Raymond! Leave her alone!"

The man's hand froze in midair. He and Bekah looked up at Mr. Harvey, who was standing behind Bekah, a big shovel in his hand. The one Bekah had seen him use the night before. Mr. Harvey came toward them, his lips pressed tightly together.

Raymond laughed. "You don't scare me, old man." But he put his arm down.

"I want you off my property," Mr. Harvey said, clutching the shovel with both hands. "And I never want to see you again."

"Not until I get what's mine." Raymond stood up and went to Mr. Harvey. "You owe me, old man."

Bekah scrambled to her feet, holding her arm against her body.

"Little girl, you go on home now." Mr. Harvey spoke to Bekah, but his gaze remained on Raymond, unflinching. "You run home and lock your doors. You hear?"

She didn't say anything, just turned around and ran. The

tears she had held in squeezed out of her eyes. She raced to the back door, yelling in frustration when she found the door locked. "Amanda! Amanda let me in."

A few seconds later the door opened. Amanda grabbed Bekah's good arm and yanked her inside. Then her arms went around her. "Thank God you're all right."

Bekah couldn't speak. The fear that had kept her from falling apart still had its grip on her. She stepped back and looked at Amanda.

"What did he do to your arm?" Amanda asked.

"I don't know, but it hurts really bad." Suddenly she heard a faraway voice calling out Amanda's name. She looked down to see that Amanda was holding her father's cell phone. Her cousin put it against her ear. "It's okay, *Daed*. Bekah's here." Amanda smiled, her lips trembling slightly. "You were right. Prayer does work."

Bekah's arm ached as she watched Amanda talk to her father. After a short conversation she put her hand over the mouthpiece. "*Daed* wants me to stay on the line with him until *Onkel* Thomas comes home."

She thought that made sense. Through the open window in the living room she could hear shouting next door. She motioned for Amanda to follow her upstairs. They went to her bedroom and watched Mr. Harvey and Raymond yelling at each other. Mr. Harvey was still holding up the shovel. Bekah was worried for him. While he had yelled at her, he wasn't *ab im kopp* like Raymond was. At least, she didn't think so. He had saved her, after all.

The men were screaming at each other, but she couldn't make out what they were saying. Raymond had his hands up in the air, pacing back and forth like he had when he'd kept Bekah in the kitchen. Suddenly he lunged at Mr. Harvey. Bekah sucked in a breath. But at that same moment Mr. Harvey brought the shovel down hard on Raymond's shoulder. The younger man's legs buckled from the blow and he went to his knees.

She gasped and looked at Amanda, who was still talking to her father but in low tones. She realized she wasn't even watching Raymond and Mr. Harvey. She was involved in her conversation with her *daed*. For the first time since she had come to Paradise, Bekah saw Amanda genuinely smile. Despite the pain in her arm and the fight between Mr. Harvey and Raymond, she couldn't help but smile too.

In the distance she heard the sound of sirens. "Did you call the police?" she asked Amanda.

Amanda pulled the phone from her ear. "*Ya*. *Daed* told me to."

Bekah breathed a sigh of relief and looked out the window again. Raymond was still on his knees, clutching his shoulder. Mr. Harvey had the shovel raised in front of him, but even from this distance she could see he was unsteady. The shovel quaked in his arms, and he looked like he was ready to drop it at any moment.

Never had she been so relieved when she saw the police car pull into the driveway. Normally, the Amish didn't get involved with the police, preferring to handle problems within the community. But in this case, Bekah said a thankful prayer that they had shown up so quickly. The officers exited the car, the blue lights flashing on top. They went to the backyard where Raymond and Mr. Harvey were. One officer went to Raymond, pulling him up by his good arm. The other stood by Mr. Harvey, taking the shovel from him. The old man staggered backward, and the police officer took his arm, steadying him.

"Bekah! Amanda!"

At the sound of her mother's voice, Bekah looked at Amanda. Amanda told her father good-bye and hung up the phone just as her mother ran inside their room, not bothering to knock as she usually did.

"What on earth is going on?" Her face was pale with fright. "Your father and I just got home. Why are the police over at Mr. Harvey's *haus*?" Then she turned to Bekah. "*Dochder*, you're white as a sheet."

At that moment, the weight of the morning overwhelmed Bekah; she couldn't take it anymore. All the fear and the tears released within her. She ran to her mother and put her arms around her, not caring about the pain piercing her arm. "Oh, *Mami*. I'm so sorry. I'm so very, very sorry."

Bekah winced, but she didn't dare cry out as her mother put her arm in a makeshift sling, which was an old pillowcase holding her arm in place and tied in a knot at her shoulder. Her mother and father were angry enough, and with good reason. Bekah hadn't even told them the whole story yet. Just knowing she had disobeyed them by going over to Mr. Harvey's was enough to upset them.

Her father sat down at the table, not saying anything. But his silence spoke enough to her. She'd never seen her father this grim before, not even when *Onkel* Ezra had dropped off Amanda. Bekah glanced up at her mother, who was securing the knot. Her cheeks were the shade of overripe strawberries. Amanda's expression wasn't much better, although instead of anger, she sat very still in the chair, her eyes wide with fear. Dread swirled inside Bekah. She could only imagine what her punishment would be.

Her mother finished the knot, then sat down. All four of them remained quiet. The cell phone was in the middle of the table. Suddenly it rang, causing all of them to jump.

Daed answered it. "Hello? *Ya*, Ezra. Everything is all right. I'm still not sure what happened . . . oh, you are? That's fine. I'm sure she'll be happy to see you. All right. I'll let her know." He hung up the phone and looked at Amanda. His expression wasn't happy. "Your father is coming to see you tomorrow. He should be here sometime in the afternoon."

Amanda's face lit up, but quickly faded. "But tomorrow's Sunday. Won't he get in trouble for traveling here on the Lord's day?"

Bekah thought Amanda had a good point. Sundays were for worship and rest. No work, other than taking care of the animals, was to be done. Her mother didn't even cook on Sunday, making food ahead of time on Saturday, or they just ate sandwiches and other cold foods for lunch and supper.

Bekah's father shrugged. "That's up to him. I think he'd take the risk to come here and make sure you are okay. You gave him quite a scare." He looked at Bekah. "You both did."

Nodding, Bekah said, "I'm sorry, *Daed*. It's my fault, not Amanda's. She didn't want to *geh* to Mr. Harvey's. I did."

"But why?" her mother said. "Why would you do the exact opposite of what we asked you to do? You're not a disobedient *kinn*, Bekah. What got into you?"

Bekah looked down at her lap. She was hurting and embarrassed. And wrong. Looking back, she'd made so many mistakes the past few weeks, all because she was too nosy for her own good. "I don't know." But she did; she just couldn't admit it. She should have never gone to Mr. Harvey's in the first place. She should have never snooped around his yard, or spied on him while he was digging holes in his yard. She shouldn't have told Miriam or Caleb about what she saw. She should have gone straight to her parents, instead of trying to solve the mystery herself. After what happened with Raymond, she was lucky a sore arm was the only thing that happened to her. It could have been so much worse.

A knock sounded on the front door. Her father, still scowling, got up and left the kitchen. He came back a few moments later with a police officer. The man was tall, his head nearly hitting the low ceiling in their house. She looked up at him, and he caught her gaze. His brown eyes softened a bit.

"I think you're the young lady I'm looking for. I want to ask you a few questions about what happened to you." He paused, looking at her father, then to her mother. "If that's all right with your parents."

Her father gave him a curt nod. "But you'll ask them here, and my wife and I will be here too."

The police officer nodded. "Do you mind if I sit down?"

Her mother stood up as her father pulled out a chair for the officer. "Do you want anything to drink?" she asked.

Bekah wasn't surprised that her mother would offer hospitality. That was the Amish way.

But the officer shook his head. "No thanks, ma'am. I want to make this as quick and painless as possible. Your name, please?" He pulled a small notebook out of his shirt pocket.

"Bekah Yoder."

"Rebekah," her mother corrected, smiling.

The policeman smiled too, then looked at Bekah's arm. "You're injured?"

"Just my shoulder."

"What happened?"

Bekah fought to keep her nerves steady. The police officer seemed kind, but she had never spoken to the police before. She looked to her father, who nodded to her, giving her a small but encouraging smile. It helped, and she was able to find her voice. "When that man—Raymond is what Mr. Harvey called him—kept me in the *haus*, he grabbed my arm and folded it behind my back." Even thinking about it intensified the pain in her arm.

Her mother let out a squeak. Bekah turned to see her standing at the stove, her fingertips over her mouth. She was turning on the stove with a shaky hand.

The officer frowned, taking notes on the small paper with a ballpoint pen. "Why don't we start from the beginning."

Bekah told him everything, from finding the first hole with Caleb to Raymond kidnapping her and making her dig for the money. "But I didn't know what he was talking about," she said. "I never saw any money. I thought maybe Mr. Harvey was burying some kind of treasure, but I never found any."

"So you dug up his yard while he wasn't home?"

She glanced down at her lap again. "*Ya*."

"Do you realize that's considered trespassing?"

Bekah lifted her head and nodded. Tears overflowed her eyes and trickled down her cheeks.

The officer frowned, shifting in his seat. His lips beneath his light brown mustache thinned out. "From what you're telling me, Mr. Harvey didn't want you on his property. Neither did your parents."

"I know. I'm sorry. And ashamed." Then she felt a hand on her good shoulder. She looked up to see Amanda standing next to her.

"This wasn't all her fault," Amanda said. "I was over there too. I went to get a shovel to dig up his yard. I wanted to know what he was burying over there. So you can't just get mad at Bekah."

"This is my niece, Amanda Yoder," Bekah's father said sternly.

"Thank you, sir," the officer said. Then he looked at the girls again. "I'm not mad at either of you." He flipped his book closed. "I can't say the same for your parents, or for Mr. Harvey. Raymond Harvey is a very dangerous man, and old Mr. Harvey knew that. That's probably why he wanted you to keep away from him. He knew his son had escaped from prison, and it was likely he would try to find him. That's why he had moved here to Middlefield, and to the house next door. He never thought his son would find him on a rural road in the middle of Amish country."

Bekah's eyes grew wide. Raymond was Mr. Harvey's son? She could hardly believe it.

The teakettle whistled, and Bekah looked to see her mother turn off the gas. "It would have been *gut* if he would have told us that," she said in a low but upset tone.

"Margaret," Bekah's father warned.

She took a deep breath and looked at him. She nodded, then went to sit down in one of the chairs next to him.

Bekah's father put his hands on the table and clasped his fingers together. "So what happens next?"

"Raymond will be taken back to jail in Pennsylvania. I'm sure the district attorney will press additional charges of kidnapping and assaulting your daughter. That's provided you will be willing to cooperate with the Pennsylvania authorities." He leaned forward and looked at Bekah's father. "I have to be honest, they'll probably want your daughter to testify. Which means Rebekah will have to appear in court. Amanda probably will too."

But her father was already shaking his head. "We won't press charges. Or testify. We're a peaceful people. I don't want my family involved in any of that." He looked at Bekah. "We forgive Raymond for what he did to Bekah, just as we hope Mr. Harvey will forgive the girls for trespassing."

The officer nodded. "That's what I thought you'd say. I'll let Mr. Harvey know. Even though he's upset with his son, he's concerned for him as well."

"What about his shoulder?" Bekah asked.

"Whose shoulder?" The officer asked, turning to Bekah.

"Raymond's. His *daed* hit him in the shoulder with the shovel."

The officer shrugged. "Neither of them said anything about that. We saw Mr. Harvey holding a shovel when we arrived, and considering Raymond's agitated state, we don't blame him for wanting to protect himself. Raymond was holding his shoulder when we put him in the squad car, but he didn't say that anyone attacked him."

Bekah was surprised Raymond didn't tell the police that his father had hit him. He was so mean, she wouldn't put it past him to try to get his father in trouble. But maybe there was hope for him after all.

Eighteen

LATER THAT evening Bekah and Amanda were in their room, lying on the bed. It wasn't time to go to sleep, but they had both been sent to their room shortly after the police officer had left. Bekah knew her parents were downstairs discussing her punishment, which would undoubtedly be severe. She fully expected the worst. After everything she had done, she deserved it.

Both girls lay on their backs, looking at the ceiling. Her shoulder throbbed, but she would have to deal with it. She wouldn't be able to go to a doctor until at least Monday, and that's if they could get an appointment. Her mother said her arm wasn't swollen, and that it was probably just sprained. Bekah had broken a finger two years ago when she fell down running around the playground at school. That pain didn't compare to how her shoulder felt. But it was just one of many repercussions she had to experience because of her bad decisions.

She turned her head and looked at Amanda. Her cousin was staring up at the ceiling too. Guilt slashed through Bekah. It was her fault they were in trouble, even though Amanda had tried to shoulder some of the blame. "I'm sorry," she said.

Amanda shrugged. "We were both over there. I could have just gone back home."

"But you didn't. And if I hadn't dragged you into this, you wouldn't be in trouble."

"Well, maybe not as much." She looked at Bekah. "How's the shoulder?"

"Sore." They fell silent for a moment, then Bekah spoke again. "I really am sorry. For everything. I should have believed that you didn't say anything to Caleb. I told Miriam about the holes, but . . . I didn't think she'd tell. She promised me she wouldn't." She sighed.

"I didn't want to say anything," Amanda said, "but I did see her and Caleb talking right after school that day. She likes him, doesn't she?"

"*Ya*. I don't know why, but she does."

Amanda nodded. "It's pretty obvious. But it's also obvious he doesn't like her. He has his eye on someone else."

Bekah scowled. "Let me guess. Me."

She grinned. "So you see it too."

"*Nee*, I don't. But you're not the first one to tell me that. It doesn't matter, because I will never like him."

"Never say never."

Bekah laughed, then stopped and grimaced. It even

hurt to laugh. "Are you excited about your father coming tomorrow?"

"*Ya*. I'm really happy." She put her arm behind her head, making her kerchief slide forward a bit. "I wasn't sure he'd ever come back for me."

"You didn't really believe that, did you?"

She nodded. "I did." She didn't say anything for a moment, and when she finally did speak it was in a whisper. "My *mamm* left us."

Bekah pretended to be surprised. "Why would she do that?"

"I don't know. And I didn't want to tell anyone here about it. I didn't want people to know my *mamm* didn't want me."

"That can't be true." Bekah slowly sat up, resting her arm against her chest. She angled her body toward Amanda. "Maybe her leaving had nothing to do with you. Or your *daed*."

"Then why else would she *geh*?" Tears pooled in Amanda's eyes, and she wiped them away. Then she sat up. "I don't care what her reasons are. I just want her back. And I know she's coming back."

"How do you know?"

She looked at Bekah, looking more peaceful than Bekah had ever seen her. "Because God answers prayer. I found that out today. But I haven't always been so sure. Ever since I've been here, I've prayed every night for my *mamm* and *daed* to get back together and come get me. But day after day I didn't hear anything. And I gave up on him, I did. But then when I saw you with Raymond, I called *Daed,* and he told me to pray harder than I ever had. And I did. As soon as I said amen, Mr. Harvey showed up."

Bekah's eyes grew round. "Wow."

"*Ya*. And now my *daed* says he's coming to get me tomorrow. That's a second answer to prayer. So I know God is hearing me. I'll keep praying for my *mamm* to come back, and eventually she will."

Touching Amanda's arm with her good hand, Bekah said, "I'll pray the same thing."

The girls heard Bekah's father calling to them from downstairs. They looked at each other, both gulping at the same time. "I guess this is it," Bekah said.

"*Ya*."

Neither of them moved. Bekah's father called one more time.

"We'd better go," Bekah said. "Or else we'll get into more trouble."

Amanda scrambled off the bed while Bekah gingerly scooted off of it. A sickening lump formed in her stomach. She didn't care what her punishment was, but she didn't want to face her parents. She hated to see the disappointment in their eyes.

She followed Amanda downstairs, stopping at the base of the stairs right behind her. In addition to her parents standing in the middle of the room, there was someone else there too.

"Bekah. Amanda." Bekah's *daed* moved toward them. "Mr. Harvey wants to talk to you."

Bekah couldn't move. She was almost as afraid as she'd been when Raymond captured her. She looked at Amanda. Her cousin's expression mirrored her own.

"Girls." Her mother came over to them. "Come sit down. We don't want to keep Mr. Harvey waiting."

Mr. Harvey sat down on the chair opposite the couch while the girls sat down across from him. It was strange seeing him this close up. He still had more wrinkles than Bekah had ever seen before, and his eyes had a yellowish tinge to them. But they were also filled with sadness. Bekah found herself feeling sorry for him, which surprised her. She would have expected him to be angry with her.

"I think Bekah and Amanda have something to tell you, Mr. Harvey." Bekah's father sat down next to his wife on the other end of the couch. He looked at Bekah and Amanda. "Right, girls?"

They both nodded, and Bekah spoke first. "Mr. Harvey, I'm really sorry for trespassing in your yard. I should have minded my own business. I'm also sorry for spying on you."

He leaned forward in the chair. "You were spying on me?"

She nodded, her cheeks heating with embarrassment. "I saw you digging in your yard. I thought you were burying treasure or something like that." She didn't dare say anything about the bones.

Rubbing his grizzled chin with one finger, he looked at her. She couldn't tell if he was angry or not. Then he broke out in a grin. "I'll be. The last thing I thought I'd have to worry about when I moved out here was some Amish girl spying on me in the middle of the night."

"I assure you Bekah will face the consequences for what she did," her father said. "Also, if she ruined your yard she will pay to have it repaired."

This time Mr. Harvey laughed. It transformed him from a crabby old man to someone who seemed like he could almost be kind. "Don't worry about that. I dug so many holes in that yard I ruined it myself. As far as consequences . . . I think her run-in with Raymond has taught her enough of a lesson."

Bekah was surprised. "You do?"

"Yep. But far be it from me to tell your folks what to do. That's up to them how they discipline you. I sure don't have the right to be giving parenting advice." His expression dimmed. "Didn't do such a great job with my own boy."

"I'm sorry." Bekah didn't know why those words came to her lips. But she was.

He held up his hand. "No need to be sorry about that. Long ago I accepted my son had problems I couldn't understand or handle. I came over here to apologize to you girls and to your parents. I should have told you that my son had escaped from jail and that he might be coming. But I'd hoped he wouldn't find me out here. I guess I should have known better; I'm the first person he hunts down when he needs something." He looked at her parents. "I hope you can forgive me for that someday."

Her father's stern expression softened. "No need to ask. It's already forgotten."

"Thank you. I'd always been told you people were the forgiving type. My cousin Alma used to own this house. I bought it from her last year and planned to move here from Pittsburgh soon after. But my wife got sick . . ." He wiped at his eyes, then lifted his head. "It was a long illness."

"I'm so sorry," Bekah's mother said.

"Thank you. Took awhile before I could get out here after that. Then I'm on my way, and I get a phone call from the police saying Raymond's escaped. I'd already pulled up stakes in Pittsburgh. I couldn't go back after that. When I got here, I thought if I kept to myself it would be all right. If Raymond came after me, at least he wouldn't hurt no one else." He looked at Bekah. "I'm sorry he did that to you. My boy, he's not so nice."

Bekah couldn't believe how kind Mr. Harvey was being. He didn't seem mad about anything she'd done; instead, he was more upset that she was hurt.

Mr. Harvey ran his palms down the front of his brown pants. "Raymond knows I always keep a little money stashed for a rainy day. I suspect that's what he was looking for. I decided to keep what I've got, plus some papers and other things, in a chest. They used to bury valuables back in the old days. I figured he'd never suspect that I was doing that with my things. Guess I should have just gotten a safety-deposit box, like everyone else does."

"He did keep asking me where the money was," Bekah said. "I told him I didn't know."

"What were you doing in the backyard, then?"

"He caught me digging back there. I was looking for . . . that chest you buried the other night."

"You saw me do that? Child, it was past midnight when I was out there that night."

"Which explains why you've been so tired," her mother interjected.

"*Ya, Mami.* I stayed up to watch Mr. Harvey bury a big chest in his backyard. I couldn't figure out why he was digging all these small holes and then one big hole."

"It's not your place to figure that out."

"I know."

"Well," Mr. Harvey said. "Can't blame someone for being curious. I probably would have done the same thing if I'd seen some old man burying something in the backyard when I was a kid." His gaze narrowed. "Not that it would have been right for me to do it either."

"I understand."

He rose from his chair. "That's it, I suppose. I just wanted to check on you, uh . . ."

"Bekah." Bekah stood up too. "And this is my cousin Amanda. She's visiting from Paradise."

"Well then, I guess you got you some stories to tell your friends when you get back." Mr. Harvey turned to Bekah's parents. "Thanks for letting me come over and apologize for myself and my son. I'm hoping he'll get the help he needs while he's in jail."

Her father held out his hand. "We'll pray that he does."

Mr. Harvey's bottom lip shook for a brief moment. "I,

uh, appreciate that," he said, his voice sounding thick. He dipped his head toward Bekah's mother. "Ma'am."

"Mr. Harvey." Her mother stepped forward. "We're just getting ready to have supper. Would you like to join us?"

He shook his head. "I wouldn't want to impose."

"You're not imposing. We've got plenty. Amanda, come help me with supper. We'll set the table for five tonight instead of four."

Amanda nodded and left the room. Mr. Harvey looked down at the floor, scuffing his toe against the wood floor. "Only if you're sure."

"We insist," Bekah's father said. "We should have done this right after you moved in."

"I wouldn't have come. I didn't want to get anyone involved in my problems."

"Mr. Harvey, that's what neighbors are for." He turned to Bekah. "*Geh* help Amanda and your mother. But make sure you watch that arm."

Bekah nodded. "I will." She headed for the kitchen, but her father's voice stopped her.

"Listen to me this time."

She took a deep breath. "Always, *Daed*. From now on, I always will."

Nineteen

THE NEXT day Bekah and her family went to church. In all the excitement of what had happened yesterday, she had forgotten it was Caleb's family's time to host church. On the way to his house, she tried to steel herself for an entire day of Caleb Mullet, since her family usually stayed behind for lunch afterward. Even though they could walk over to the Mullets, her father had insisted on taking the buggy because of Bekah's arm.

Her arm didn't hurt as badly that morning. It wasn't until her father was turning into the Mullets' driveway that the realization she was going to church with a pillowcase wrapped around her arm dawned on her—one more consequence of her bad choices.

They had arrived just in time for the service, so she didn't have to speak to anyone until after it was over. But then she was bombarded by her friends, some of them who had already heard rumors about what had happened.

"I heard they sent four police cars."

"Is it true that the guy had a gun?"

"Someone said you hit him over the head with a shovel."

Bekah refuted each outlandish claim with the truth. "None of that happened. Someone tried to rob Mr. Harvey, and he saw me and thought I knew where Mr. Harvey kept the money."

"Then how did you hurt your arm?" Ester asked, her eyes filled with wonder and sympathy.

"The man did. He wasn't very nice. But everything turned out okay. That's all that happened." And it was, the shortened version. Her friends didn't need to know the complete truth.

"But I want to know how—"

"Who wants to play a game of volleyball?" Amanda stepped forward. "We've got enough here for two teams. Except for Bekah, of course."

"I'll be happy to watch." She looked at Amanda, grateful to her for saving her from more questions. Amanda winked at her and faced her friends. "I'll be one captain, and . . ." She looked at the group and stopped when her gaze landed on Melvin. "You can be the other."

"All right." Melvin grinned. "If that's the case, I'll take Caleb."

Caleb stepped forward. "I'm sitting this one out too."

"Oh, c'mon. You're our best player."

Caleb shook his head. "I'll get the next game."

"Fine. I'll take Ester, then."

"Wait," Amanda said, going after Melvin as the kids ran

to the volleyball net set up in the Mullets' backyard. "When do I get to pick someone?"

Ester hung back and looked at Bekah. "Your cousin's come out of her shell, hasn't she?"

Bekah shrugged. "I knew it would happen someday."

Ester grinned and ran over to the other kids. Bekah smiled as she watched them divvy up teams. She had forgotten Caleb was standing next to her until he cleared his throat.

"Why aren't you out there playing?" Bekah asked.

"Because I wanted to talk to you."

Great. Here we go again. "I thought you said you were going to leave me alone."

"I said I wasn't going to play any more practical jokes on you."

"That's the same thing."

"I don't think so." A serious look crossed his face. "I want to know what really happened."

"I already told you." She turned and walked away from him, toward the pond at the back of the Mullets' property. She passed by the volleyball game and saw Amanda laughing as she missed a ball. It was good to see her cousin happy again.

"You can't just walk away from me." Caleb sidled along beside her, his pace matching hers.

"I can, and I did." But her words didn't have as much bite as they usually did. For some reason she didn't have the desire to get into an argument with him. After what she'd been through, Caleb Mullet's behavior toward her wasn't worth getting upset about.

He didn't say anything to that. They walked to the pond, and Bekah sat down under a tree at the edge of the bank. She tucked her legs beneath her and looked at the rippling pond water. "Whatever you do, don't trick me into falling into that pond."

Caleb sat down next to her. "I'm not. I told you I'm done with the *dumm* practical jokes." He lifted one knee and rested his arm on top of it. He had his Sunday best on—black pants, crisp white shirt, a black vest, and a black hat. "I'm sorry for doing all that stuff. Johnny was right. I was a *dummkopf*."

Bekah blinked. She never thought she'd ever see the day Caleb would apologize to her. "I don't know what to say."

"*Danki* is a start."

"Don't push it."

He grinned. "All right. Now, are you going to tell me what really happened?"

She looked at him. There was no teasing glint in his eye. It was the most serious she'd ever seen him—or else he was the best liar she'd ever met. "If there's one thing I learned from all this, being nosy can get you into trouble. Big trouble."

"I'm not being nosy."

"*Ya*, you are."

He looked at her. "I'm concerned, all right?" Then he glanced down, his cheeks slightly reddening.

Bekah's brows lifted. "Really?"

"Really. Just don't make me admit it again. I have a reputation to keep."

It was her turn to smile. "I heard you the first time. But before I tell you anything, I need to know who spilled about the holes in Mr. Harvey's yard."

He let out a deep breath. "Miriam. But don't be too mad at her."

"Why not? She promised she wouldn't tell anyone! I actually thought Amanda was the one who told."

Caleb dropped his knee and sat cross-legged. He started pulling at the grass. "I saw you and Miriam whispering to each other, and I took a chance that you were talking about the old man—"

"Mr. Harvey."

"Right. Mr. Harvey. Anyway, I know she kind of likes me, so I convinced her to tell me what you said."

"Caleb Mullet, that was sneaky. And not a nice thing to do."

"I know, I know. If it's worth anything, I felt guilty about it and apologized to her. So like I said, don't get mad at her. Get mad at me. I'm used to it anyway."

But Bekah couldn't be mad at him. Not anymore. "It's all right. Considering the *dumm* things I did, that's nothing." And she proceeded to tell him what had happened, in much more detail than she had given her friends. When she was finished, Caleb was wide-eyed.

"Wow. So Mr. Harvey's son escaped from jail, kidnapped you, sprained your arm, and made you dig for money that you knew nothing about?"

Bekah nodded.

"That's a crazy story. No wonder you didn't want to tell."

"*Ya*. And I don't want them to know all that. You have to keep everything I told you to yourself." She narrowed her gaze. "I don't know if I can trust you to do that, though. I haven't had much luck with secrets lately. In fact, I don't think keeping secrets is a such a *gut* idea."

"Depends on the secret." Caleb looked at the pond. "Look, I know my word probably means as much to you as that clod of dirt over there, but I promise I won't say a word to anyone. If I do, you have my permission to *geh* straight to Johnny and tell him. Believe me, he'll let me have it. I think he lives to put me in my place sometimes."

"I guess that's what big brothers do. Or so I've heard."

"*Ya*." He tossed a blade of grass in the air and it floated to the ground. "So did Mr. Harvey ever tell you what he buried?"

"*Ya*. He told us over dinner that night." She adjusted her arm in the sling, then leaned back against the tree, smiling.

He looked over his shoulder, glancing down at her. "Are you going to tell me?"

"Someday."

He jumped to his feet. "That's not fair, Bekah Yoder."

She grinned. "I know."

For the first time since she'd attended school in Middlefield, Amanda had a good day. She'd had so much fun on Sunday playing volleyball with the other kids, and almost all of them went to her school. They greeted her when she arrived at school, and two girls her own age invited her to eat lunch with them. It felt so nice to be around them, and it made her forget about her father, who hadn't shown up Sunday like he promised. He had called, explaining he couldn't get a bus ticket in time, but that he would be there today. She was excited to see him, but she had mixed feelings about that.

Bekah said her shoulder was feeling better too, and when they got home from school, *Aenti* Margaret said she didn't think Bekah needed to go to the doctor. Bekah and Amanda settled at the kitchen table with their homework, each of them with a glass of milk and two snickerdoodle cookies.

"I saw the buggy parked in front of the barn," Bekah said. "Did *Daed* come home early?"

"*Ya*. He hired a driver and went to the bus station to pick up *Onkel* Ezra." Amanda saw Bekah looking at her. "Your father should be on his way."

Amanda smiled, but her emotions were mixed. She wanted to see her father more than anything, but she would miss being here. A month ago she would have never believed she'd feel that way, but a lot had happened since she arrived. When she first came to Middlefield, she had almost nothing, and very little hope. She felt abandoned by everyone, including God. Now she felt more accepted and loved than she thought possible.

They had just finished their homework when the back door opened. Amanda jumped up from her chair just as her father walked into the kitchen. "*Daed*!"

He scooped her up in his arms, hugging her tight. "I've missed you so much," he whispered in her ear.

She leaned her head against his shoulder for a second, then he put her down. He stepped back from her. "You're looking thin," he said, frowning, then looking at *Aenti* Margaret.

"It's not *Aenti*'s fault. I wouldn't eat when I first got here."

His eyes became glassy. "I should have never left you. I'm sorry, *lieb*. I thought I was doing the right thing."

"You did, *Daed*." She looked up at her father. They'd only been apart for a month, but he looked different. Older. More tired. Maybe he had lost his hope too. Her heart went out to him. "I'm glad I got to stay here. *Aenti* Margaret and *Onkel* Thomas have been so *gut* to me. And I've had a great time with Bekah."

Her *daed* smirked. "So I've heard. I'm glad you called me that day. I just wish I could have done more."

Onkel Thomas put his hand on his brother's shoulder. "I'll take your bag upstairs. You'll be staying in Katherine's room. She's bunking down here."

He shook his head. "I can't take my niece's room."

"It's all right," *Aenti* Margaret said. "She's been working so many hours lately we rarely see her."

Amanda saw her uncle gesture with his head to her aunt and Bekah. They quickly disappeared, leaving Amanda and her father in the kitchen.

They both sat down at the table. Her father looked at her, his expression intense. "Amanda, I have something to tell you."

"Can I tell you something first?" Excitement colored her tone.

His reddish brow lifted. "All right. You sound like you're about to pop. What is it?"

She grinned. "*Mamm*'s coming back!"

He leaned back from her, shock on his face. "How do you know that? Has she been in touch with you?"

Amanda shook her head. "*Nee*."

"Then what makes you so sure?"

"Because of what you said."

He gave his head a hard shake. "What I said?"

"When Bekah was in trouble, you told me to pray as hard as I could, and I did. Right after that Mr. Harvey showed up and saved Bekah."

"That's *gut*, Amanda, but—"

"And all the while I've been here, I've prayed you would come back. And here you are. So I've been praying that *Mamm* would come back to us, and we would be a family again. Bekah's been praying for that too. We figure two prayers should be better than one, right?"

Her *daed* tilted his head to the side. He reached out and touched her cheek. "The faith of a *kinn*. It's a wonderful thing."

"What does that mean?"

"Never mind." He dropped his hand and leaned forward. "I need you to listen to me carefully, Amanda. I want you to understand what I'm going to tell you. It's important."

She nodded, ready to hear what he had to say.

"God doesn't always answer our prayers, at least in the ways we think he should."

Amanda frowned. That wasn't what she had expected him to say. "I don't understand."

"What I'm trying to say is that God is always faithful. He'll never leave us alone. Even when we think we're alone, he's always there. Caring for us. Loving us. And he wants our prayers. He wants us to go to him and ask for things. To tell him how much we love him and appreciate what he does. Like you said, he hears our prayers. And he answers them. But he answers them in the ways that are best for us."

She was trying to understand what he meant. "Are you saying that *Mamm* isn't coming back?"

He leaned back in the chair and sighed.

Amanda's eyes stung with tears. It was as if all the hope she'd stored in her heart the past few days leaked out, leaving her empty again. "Why isn't she coming back?"

"Because she's not ready. Your *mamm* has depression, Amanda. Do you know what that means?"

"I know she was sad a lot before she left."

"Right. And sometimes there's so much sadness inside her that she can't think about anything else."

Amanda understood what that meant. She had felt that for most of her time in Middlefield.

"But the *gut* news is that she's willing to see someone who will help her. Right now she's at a hospital in Lancaster." He put his hands on her shoulders. "She misses you, Amanda. And she loves you. She wants to come back to us. It's just going to take some time."

Amanda smiled, her spirits lifting again. She would have her mother back again. Just like the Lord had promised.

Two days later Bekah waved to Amanda as she and her father left in a taxi for the bus station. She fought the lump in her throat. She would miss Amanda, more than she ever thought possible. In a way it wasn't fair—they were just now getting to be friends. But Amanda wanted to go back to Paradise with her father and visit her mother in the hospital. Bekah had promised she would keep praying that Amanda's mother would get better, so they could be a family again. Her parents had also promised she could visit Amanda in Paradise this summer. She had something to look forward to.

Her parents had gone back inside, but Bekah wasn't ready to just yet. She went to the swing set and sat down. Her arm was still in the sling, but that was more at her mother's insistence—her shoulder barely hurt anymore. Still, she kept her arm still and only leaned her body back and forth in the swing. She heard a bark and lifted her head. She laughed as she saw Roscoe coming toward her; she could tell he had something in his mouth. Again. "Come here, *bu*." Roscoe dropped the bone at her feet, then sat down and let her pet him.

"That dog's at it again, isn't he?"

Bekah looked up to see Mr. Harvey, who was walking toward her. "I'm afraid so, Mr. Harvey."

"Blasted dog. He's been hanging around my house all day long."

She smiled and scratched Roscoe's ear. "Because he likes you."

"He likes my yard, that's what. I wish whoever is giving him those steak bones would stop. It has to be someone close by. Maybe the fellow who owns that herd down the road."

"*Herr* Troyer?" Bekah looked in the direction of the Troyer farm. "He might be."

"If he is, I'll have to ask him to stop." Mr. Harvey stopped in front of her, crossing his arms over his thin chest. When Roscoe turned and barked at him, he frowned. "I'm tired of him burying those bones in my yard."

Bekah laughed. "How long do you think he's been doing it?"

Mr. Harvey shrugged. "Long before I moved in. I'm surprised you never saw him do it, considering how curious you are." His lips twitched, like he was about to smile but couldn't bring himself to do it.

Bekah dragged her toe across the ground. She needed to ask Mr. Harvey a question, but she wasn't sure if she should. While she didn't find him scary anymore—he was actually pretty nice—she had learned her lesson about being nosy. But that didn't stop her from being curious.

"Something on your mind?"

She looked up. Mr. Harvey gave her a half smile, which bolstered her courage. If he thought she was being nosy, then he'd tell her. He wasn't one to mince words. "*Ya*. I wondered if I could ask you something."

"Sure."

"But before I do I want to apologize again for spying on you." Her cheeks reddened. "I promise I won't spy again, but may I ask what was in all of the smaller holes?"

To her surprise, Mr. Harvey chuckled. "Suppose you wouldn't be normal if you weren't curious about an old man burying stuff in his backyard. As far as those holes . . ." His smile faded. "It's probably going to sound silly to a child like you, but I was burying letters."

"Letters?"

"Yep. Letters from my son. He wasn't always bad, you know. He was a great kid. We loved to go fishing together on Saturday mornings. Then when he got in high school, he fell into the wrong crowd. After that he was never the same. When he was in prison, he would write me hateful letters. I saved every one, but I never showed them to my wife."

Bekah stopped swinging, feeling bad for Mr. Harvey. "Why did you save them?"

"Didn't really know at the time." He rubbed his finger underneath his bottom lip. "But when I got here, I knew it was time to let go of those letters, just like I had to let go of my son. So I buried them. Then I prayed for him. I still pray for him every day." He averted his gaze and shook his head. Then he looked at her again. "But enough of that. No more burying stuff in the yard. And no more secrets. Things will be mighty boring around here from now on."

Bekah glanced at her arm. "I'm okay with that . . . for a while anyway."

Mr. Harvey chuckled again. "Good to know. So is that Mullet boy still pestering you to tell him what's in my backyard?"

She nodded. "*Ya.*"

"Are you ever going to tell him?"

"Would you be mad if I did?"

He shook his head. "Nah. I don't have anything to hide anymore."

"Then maybe I will." She twisted in the swing and smirked. "Or maybe I won't."

He shook his head and turned around. "I'll never understand you young people."

"Good night, Mr. Harvey."

He lifted his hand and waved without turning around.

Bekah smiled. Maybe she'd drop a couple more hints to Caleb the next time she saw him. Just a few to get him curious. She had to admit it was fun to frustrate Caleb. For some reason he didn't seem to mind it too much. Maybe her cousin was right—Caleb Mullet wasn't all that bad after all.

Look for Book Three
in The Mysteries of Middlefield Series

Hide and Secret

One

"YOU CAN'T catch me!" Anna Mae Shetler yelled over her shoulder at her friends Amos Miller and Jeremiah Mullet. They boys had chased her deep into the woods behind her house. Cloudy puffs of air blew out of her mouth as she gasped for breath, inhaling the cold, crisp January air. The trees had long lost their leaves, and she dodged patches of snow that hadn't melted during the quick thaw they'd had a couple days ago. Behind her she could hear the boys catching up, and she pumped her legs as fast as she could to escape. The three of them had played chase for going on nine years, ever since they were five. And she'd always outran them.

But not this time. Anna Mae felt someone grip her

shoulder. She glanced to see Jeremiah pulling on her blue wool coat.

"Gotcha!" He yanked harder.

Just as she tried to break free, her foot slid out from underneath her and she lost her balance. She tumbled backward, sliding into the cold, wet leaves, her breath knocked out of her. Jeremiah landed beside her.

"Ooof!" he exclaimed as he hit the ground, then rolled over.

Anna Mae lifted her head, her chest heaving. She pushed herself up to a sitting position. Something tickled her cheek, and she reached up to pull off a couple of leaves stuck to her skin.

Amos lumbered toward them. He leaned forward, his hands on his knees. "Are . . . you . . . two . . . okay?"

She nodded, tossing the leaves on the ground. She wasn't hurt, just annoyed that Jeremiah had caught up to her. She looked at him, who was reaching for his hat, which had flown off his head and landed on a fallen tree nearby.

"I'm fine." He brushed a few clumps of wet snow off his hat and plopped it on his head.

Anna Mae felt the dampness of the cold ground seep through her skirt. She jumped to her feet and straightened her coat. Then she checked her black kapp, making sure it was still in place.

By this time Amos had caught his breath. He looked at Anna Mae and smirked. "Guess you're not the fastest anymore."

"I'm still faster than you." Amos had always been chunky,

and at age thirteen he was still short and stocky. Jeremiah was just the opposite, lean and tall. And fast, she had to admit, which bugged her. She looked at him, frowning at the triumphant expression on his face. "Don't get too proud. I slipped."

"After I caught up with you." He grinned, his freckled cheeks red from the cold.

Anna Mae turned from him and looked at tall, thick tree a few yards away. "Bet I can beat you to the tree house."

He moved to stand in front of her. "I'm sure you can't."

She put her hands on her waist. "I'm sure I can."

"Nee, you can't."

"Ya, I can." She couldn't help but smile. She and Jeremiah had been competitors for years, whether it was running races or playing baseball. They even competed against each other in school for who had the best grades. Right now they both had straight A's, and Anna Mae intended to keep it that way.

"I'll beat both of you!" Amos suddenly dashed off toward the tree house, moving surprisingly fast.

Anna Mae and Jeremiah looked at each other, then ran after Amos, who had already reached the tree house and was climbing the wood planks attached to the tree trunk.

Mustering a burst of speed, Anna Mae reached the steps a fraction ahead of Jeremiah and dashed up the tree. A few seconds later they were all in the tree house, gasping for breath.

Amos grinned, his round chest rising up and down rapidly. "I . . . won!"

"You had a head start!" Anna Mae shook her head. "That's not exactly fair."

"Doesn't . . . matter." Amos lifted his chin. "I still won." He started to strut around the tree house, his boots echoing against the old wood planks. His toe suddenly hit against a loose board in the back corner. He leaned forward, catching his balance at the last minute. "This needs fixing bad," he said, tapping the board with his boot. "Second time I tripped over it." He hit the board one more time with his boot, dislodging it.

"What did you do that for?" Jeremiah walked over and picked up the board.

"I didn't mean to. " Amos put his big hands in the pockets of his coat. "I didn't know it was that loose."

"It's okay. Next time I come out here I'll bring a hammer and a couple nails."

"Or I can ask my *daed* to do it." Anna Mae joined the boys. "I don't think he'd mind."

"But it's our tree haus, remember?" Jeremiah knelt down to replace the board. "No grown-ups allowed." He started to put the board back, then frowned. "What's this?"

Anna Mae glanced down. "I don't see anything but an empty space."

"Exactly. It's a space. Like a hole." Jeremiah looked up at her and Amos. "We should be seeing the ground."

Amos sniffed. His nose always ran when it was cold. "I don't get it."

Jeremiah didn't answer him. Instead he reached inside

the hole. A moment later he pulled out a long, narrow steel box.

Anna Mae's eyes widened. "What is that?"

"I don't know." Jeremiah set it on the floor. "But it's heavy."

"It don't look that heavy to me." Amos snatched it by the handle. But as he lifted it, the handle broke and the box hit the floor, the lid flying open. Coins, along with dozens of twenty, fifty, and hundred dollar bills spilled onto the wood floor.

"Whoa." Amos gasped. "Look at all that money." He looked at Anna Mae and Jeremiah, his brown eyes growing as big as his grin. "We're *rich*!"

Moriah's heart will only be safe with a man of his word.

Experience the best-selling novel that started the Hearts of Middlefield series.

izzy's
Popstar Plan
a daily devo that reads like a novel!
COMMENTS:
Maddie said......
Watch out world. Here comes Izzy Baxter ....Woooo Hoooo! (Posted Monday, 9:32 pm)
Ryan said......
Awesome! Can't wait to read the "way cool" and "off the wall" adventures of Izzy Baxter. LOL! (Posted Monday, 10:17 pm)
WOW
I ♥ music
ALEX MARESTAING